I Saw a Man Hit His Wife

I Saw a Man Hit His Wife

Mark Greenside

White Pine Press

Copyright ©1997 Mark Greenside

All rights reserved. This book, or portions thereof,
may not be reproduced in any form without permission.

This is a work of fiction. Names, characters, places,
and incidents are either the product of the author's imagination
or are used fictitiously, and any resemblance to actual persons,
living or dead, events, or locales is entirely coincidental.

Acknowledgments
Grateful acknowledgment is made to the following publications
for publishing these stories, some in slightly different form:
*The Bellingham Review, Beloit Fiction Journal, Crosscurrents,
Farmer's Market, Five Fingers Review, The Long Story,
The McGuffin, The Nebraska Review, The New Laurel Review,
Outerbridge, Soundings East, The Sun, Transfer, West Wind Review,*
and *Wind Literary Journal.* "Fathers Day" was first published
by Crossing Press in *Gifts of Our Fathers,* edited by Thomas Verny.

Publication of this book was made possible, in part,
by grants from the National Endowment for the Arts
and the New York State Council on the Arts.

Cover photograph: Cay Lang

Book design: Watershed Design

Manufactured in the United States of America

First Printing 1997

10 9 8 7 6 5 4 3 2 1

ISBN 1-877727-64-4

Published by
White Pine Press
10 Village Square • Fredonia, New York 14063

Acknowledgments

Writing is a solitary act, but it doesn't happen without other people contributing and making adjustments. In my case, I've been lucky. I've had many, many people, friends and family, pushing and encouraging me, believing in me and what I was doing often when I no longer did. They got me through the rough times and over the bumps. They kept me honest—to them and thereby, albeit unwittingly, to myself. I'm one of those who go searching for shortcuts. Sometimes I even find one. When I do, it's a surprise. Most of the time, though, I get lost, and what seems like an easy trip at the start turns out to be much harder and longer than I expected, filled with wrong ways, round-abouts, and dead ends.

This has been a long, long trip for me, and I've been lost more often than not.

I thank Kim Addonizio, Lucha Corpi, Dorianne Laux, Paula Panich, Gay Russell-Dempsey, and Fred Setterberg for reading these stories more times than anyone ought to read anything.

I thank Peggy DeCoursey, Donna Umeki, and LeRoy Votto for putting up with more mood swings and self-absorption than anyone not being paid at least two hundred dollars an hour should.

I thank Molly Giles for teaching me the meaning of craft and Anne Fox for her reading and editing skills.

And my students, especially those at the North Berkeley Senior Center, for making me do to my stories what I told them they had to do to theirs.

And Karen, Tom, and Dave Goetz for letting me live in their quiet and beautiful house and for letting me stay and leave as I needed. And for Snooky, their wonder dog, who patiently listened as I read him every version of every story I ever wrote.

And Elaine LaMattina and White Pine Press for asking me to write two more stories in what for me is record time and for accepting and publishing this work.

And I want to thank the following organizations for providing fellowships that made it possible to complete this work: Cummington Community of the Arts, the Djerassi Foundation, The Millay Colony for the Arts, the Ragdale Foundation, Saskatchewan Writers' Guild, the Ucross Foundation, Villa Montalvo (and especially Lori Wood for finding a place for me whenever there was a vacancy), the Virginia Center for Creative Arts, The Helene Wurlitzer Foundation of New Mexico, and The Corporation of Yaddo.

Finally, I want to thank Vista College, the Peralta Federation of Teachers, and the Peralta Community College District in Berkeley/Oakland, California, for allowing me to take time away from teaching to complete this work.

To my father, Ernest Greenside,
and Leigh Ann Lindgren, friend and lover,
neither of whom is here anymore,
both of whom never leave me;
and to my mother, Dorothy Kletter Greenside.

Contents

I Saw a Man Hit His Wife

What Is It with Women, Anyhow?

How did this happen to me, Lenny Cohen, fifty-two, married and divorced and remarried, with two kids I can't understand? Alice is Fanny's—the second wife's—so who cares? She's away at school studying prelaw or premed and *her* father's footing the bill, but the other one, Suzi, is mine. I walked into the living room the other day—the living room, mind you, in the daytime. On a weekday. A *school* day! A PRIVATE-SCHOOL day at twelve thousand smackers a year, and what do I see? She's lying on the couch with Oprah on tv and her eyes shut and her hand is under her jeans. I'm about to yell at her to tell her to stop when she opens her eyes, sees me, and screams:

"Da-ad, what are you doing here?"

I can't say anything. Her hand's still down her pants.

"Daaaaad!"

That night I tell Fanny all about it. "She's going to grow up and be a porn star, I swear. Remember that movie with George C. Scott—that's going to be my daughter, I know it."

"It's just a phase," Fanny says.

I look at her as if she's slipped. "A phase? What phase? What are you talking about? Are you crazy? And if she's doing this at home, what do you think she's doing out there?" I point.

"Don't worry, dear," Fanny smiles, "your little Suzi's not ready to leave you yet."

❖

What is it with women these days? This is something I've begun asking a lot.

"What is it with women?" I ask Laura, my masseuse at the club.

"What do you mean?" She digs in deeper and pinches a nerve.

"What is it with women?" I ask my mother-in-law.

She looks at me and shakes her head. "Our lives are filled with disappointments."

"Like what," I say, looking at the five-thousand-dollar kitchen I just paid for.

"I said I wanted yellow counters and you got me the green."

"Why are you doing that?" I ask Suzi the next time I surprise her in the living room with the tv on and her hands down under her jeans.

"Same reason you do," she says, not even bothering to look at me.

"Me!" I laugh. "Are you nuts!"

"Mom told me."

I go back to Fanny. "Not me," she yells after I yell at her. "*Her* mom. Her real mom. Not me."

So I call Beth for the first time in months. "Beth, what did you say? What did you tell Suzi?"

"The truth. I told her the truth."

"What truth?"

"That when you were her age you whacked-off to Annette on the Mouseketeers, and when we were married you liked to watch *Charlie's Angels* and do it in bed."

"WHACK-OFF! You said whack-off! This is what you told my daughter—that her father likes to whack-off!"

"Masturbate is the word I used. For Christ's sake, Lenny, it's normal."

◆

"What is it with women?" I ask Larry, my friend the shrink. He puts me on hold, then cuts me off.

I buzz Betty. "Betty, would you bring me some coffee, please?" She saunters into my office a few minutes later and stands there empty-handed, her arms folded across her chest and her legs slightly apart. She looks to me like a roadblock.

"Are we out?" I ask, reaching for my wallet.

"You are," she says. "Not me. I don't drink coffee."

"I know. Here's twenty. Get yourself whatever you want."

"Get it yourself."

Now what! Has she slipped too? She's been my secretary for a dozen years, and every day for those twelve years she's brought me coffee, sometimes a bagel, on my birthday a piece of homemade angel food cake. She's even gone out in the rain to get me coffee—and now this! What's the world coming to?"

"It's not in my job description," she says.

"You don't have a job description," I calmly inform her. "Your job is to do what I tell you."

"Not according to the union."

"Union! What union? Jesus Christ, Betty, there's just the two of us."

"AFSCME."

"Ask you what?"

"Very funny, Lenny."

"Lenny? What's this Lenny? What ever happened to Mr. C?"

"You call me Betty."

"It's your name. It says so on your desk."

"Lenny's yours—at least that's who that poor cute Sandy Waite used to ask for when she came in in the late afternoons for that *pro bono* special you gave her."

"Holy shit!" I spend the rest of the afternoon writing Betty's job description. My grandfather was a union leader. He worked with Dubinski. He went to jail with Dubinski. I know what these people can do. By four o'clock I finish, buzz Betty in, and give her the list with a smile. Number one says, "Make coffee for your superior"; number two says, "Show your superior proper respect"; number eighteen says, "And anything else not mentioned above that your superior requires you to do."

Betty reads it over quickly, looks at me, sneers, and walks out.

"Where are you going?"

"For a drink."

"It's only four o'clock."

"You started at noon...." Then she turns and walks out the door. She sticks her head back in and waves the job description in front of her face. "If this is on my desk tomorrow, I quit."

"Quit! Are you kidding? Betty! We've been together twelve years, you're family, I think of you as family, like my daughter and my wife, you can't quit family, Betty, you can't." Meanwhile, I'm thinking of my files, receipts, papers, forms, clients, books—how Betty knows and handles everything, how without her I'm lost. When she takes a vacation or a sick day, it's a disaster. I panic, then I get it. "It's money, isn't it? You want a raise, that's what this union stuff is all about?"

"Nooooo, Lenny." She shakes her head the same way every woman I've ever known has done. "What I want is respect—and to run this office the way it ought to be run. In case you forgot, I'm a trained professional. I have a degree in office management."

Oh God, not this. I knew she should have majored in something useless like French or the humanities. "Forgot! Betty, who paid for it? Who gave you the time off? Who encouraged you and told you to do it? I did—and it's because I respect and appreciate you."

"Yeah," she says, sliding the job description across my desk. "I can see."

That night I tell Fanny all about it. "Good for her," Fanny says, "Way to go."

"Good for her! Way to go! Whose side are you on? You're supposed to be my wife, for Christ's sake!"

"I am your wife, but sometimes you're an asshole, Len."

I call Larry. "My wife thinks I'm an asshole too," he says. "She hates me. All women hate me. I'm forming a group—you should join."

The next day Betty comes to work wearing slacks and a NOW button.

"*Now* what!" I joke.

"Now get off my back or I'll file a claim with the EEOC and raise ethical questions with the ABA, not to mention the NLRB. Ok?"

I slump back to my office and close the door. She has me so rattled I actually type my own letter to my mother-in-law, who's vacationing in Florida, and make my own reservations for lunch—and I don't even realize I'm doing it. As soon as I do, I put everything away and sneak out the side door earlier than usual and go around the corner for a drink. Then I go to the club to meet my best friend Howie so I can beat the shit out of him at racquet ball before we go and have lunch.

I get there first and put on my sweats. Howie comes in blushing and shaking his head. "What is it with women these days?" he says. I swear, it's the first thing he says to me.

"You tell me."

"No, *you* tell me. You've been married twice and you have a teenage daughter."

"Hey, buddy," shouts someone from the next aisle over, "I've been married four times and have five teenage daughters and what I could tell you, you could write on a bean."

Everyone in the locker room joins in. We've all been coming to this club for years, seen each other in the pool, the sauna, the steam room, the locker room, the track, the gym, and it's the first time most of us have said anything more to each other than "Hey." But in no time at all we agree: the world would be a much better place if women were more like men. Then I cream Howie at racquet ball and we go to lunch where we commiserate some more, and I have two more martinis.

When I get back to the office, I find a note on my desk from Betty. "Lenny... Taking a long lunch. Will be back soon—or, if not, will call and probably be in tomorrow." I call Larry.

"You think you got problems," he says before I say anything. "See a shrink."

"*You're* a shrink. I'm calling you."

"Mary's cheating on me."

"Mary! Cheating! Holy shit!" I can't even imagine with what: feather or furred; maybe scaled; a corpse. She's the nastiest, ugliest, meanest person I've ever seen or heard or talked about, and I'm a lawyer, for crying out loud. My heart sinks. If Mary can cheat—if a living, breathing being, or at least something that can be carbon-dated can sleep with *her*—my God, what can Fanny be up to?

That night after dinner, in a moment of quiet intimacy while Suzi is in her bedroom, I ask Fanny, "Have you ever cheated on me?"

"Just once."

"Once! Jesus! When!"

"Right after we were married."

"Right after! Holy shit! How soon?"

"That week."

"Oh my God, I don't believe this. The week we were married. The very same week! With who?"

"Remember the Cuban gardener at the Fontainebleau?"

"Him! He must have been seventy years old!"

"His grandson."

"He must have been fifteen."

"Seventeen."

"Seventeen! Jesus, he could barely speak English."

"But he *listened*, Lenny. He paid attention to everything I said. He heard me. He was with me. He never interrupted. He was THERE...."

"Fanny, Fanny, don't you get it? He *couldn't* understand you. He didn't *understand* a thing you said."

"Neither do you, and I married you. The least I could do was sleep with him. Had it been the other way around, you would have done the same."

Six of us show up at Larry's: Howie, Larry, and me, and three other guys I don't know, Barry, Marty, and Ben. I'm the last to arrive, and when I get there I find the five of them poring over Larry's professional collection of hundreds of sex mags and looking at porno tv. In no time at all we discover what we have in common: we all think about sex all the time and about doing it with anyone but our wives; we've all been married at least once and cheated at least once; we were all raised by mothers; have women secretaries; have had women teachers, nurses, friends, neighbors, colleagues, aunts, sisters, grandparents, nieces, and children, and none of us has a clue.

"All right," Larry says, "let's get down to it. Why don't we start by talking about differences. The differences between men and women." Howie holds up one of the magazines and points.

"Right, Howie. Besides those."

"They're always cold," Marty says. "Cold hands, cold feet, cold noses. And bad plumbing—they always have to pee."

"But great design." Howie holds up another photo and points.

"Ben, what about you, what do you think? Do you have something to share?" This is Larry at his professional best.

Ben looks around slowly at each of us. His mouth has begun to twitch. "Have you ever noticed," he asks, "how they want to know everything: how your day was–what you did–who you saw. Where? When? Why? What are they looking for, that's what I want to know. Why do they care? What's behind it, God-damn-it?" he pounds on the table. "They want every bit of us. They're never satisfied. They want too God-damned much!"

All of us sit there, stunned–the way you get when you know you've just heard the truth. Finally, Larry gets us going again. "This is good," he says, "this is good. Are there other things we can talk about?"

Howie shakes his head no. The rest of us sit there mute.

"All right," Barry says, "I've got one. I've been seeing this new girl, a graduate student, for about four months now. She's very sweet, a Botticelli face if you've ever seen one. We go to places like the foreign film festival and the ballet. We discuss Rilke, Keats, and Rimbaud. She quotes from Emily Dickinson and Virginia Woolf, even Wallace Stevens, and she's been a member of the Jane Austen Society for years. In the four months we've been seeing each other, all I do is hold her hand and peck her on the cheek good night. I won't even go up to her place afterwards for a drink or just to talk because I'm afraid I'll lose control. Then last night, while I'm pecking at her a good night, she grinds herself into me and leads me upstairs where she does me on the floor like Marilyn Chambers. Like Marilyn Fucking Chambers! And that's not all. Afterwards, she takes me into her study and shows me more toys and magazines than brother Larry over there's got and hands me a paper she's writing–something about reclaiming the sexual object and the dominant ground–and asks me to read a few pages. Who can explain such things, I ask you?"

I look over at Larry, who looks bent out of shape. The rest of us sit there dazed. We're jealous and scared–jealous that we didn't meet the Botticelli girl and Barry did, scared because she could have been any of our daughters or wives. The story confirms our worst nightmare: the women in our lives are beyond us. There's not a day that goes by that I try not to think of it, and not a day that goes by that I don't. Whenever Betty buzzes me and says, "It's your wife," I pick up the phone with trepidation, half expecting to hear Fanny say, "I'm leaving you, I don't love you anymore, you're history, it's over, I'm gone."

Instead of resolving anything, the evening has only heightened the mystery. I go home feeling even more unsure and unsettled than I was before. What is it with women, I wonder, why is it they will do anything except what we expect? I open the front door quietly and take off my shoes. I tip-toe up the stairs to the bedroom and find Fanny already in bed on her back with her eyes closed. The comforter is up around her shoulders and the tv is on very low. There's a candle flickering on her night table. "Fanny," I whisper, "you awake?"

"Mmmmmmm," she goes.

"Fanny?"

She opens her eyes. "Hi," she smiles. "How was it?"

"Good," I say, "Just fine," and I go to the bathroom to get undressed and brush my teeth. She looks great lying there, very sexy, and I'm glad she's awake because I really want to make love with her tonight and hope she wants to too. "Hey, Fanny," I call out, trying to get her into the mood, "do you ever have fantasies? You know," I laugh, "I mean sexual things?"

"Uh huh," she says, "I do."

"Like what?" I put my robe on and sit on the bed and listen as she tells me things I can hardly believe, things I never even had the nerve to *think* about. Now I'm *really* excited. I get up and turn the television off and hear a strange sound. "What is that? Do you hear it? Something's humming...."

Fanny moves under the covers, twists, and holds up a long, thin black dildo in front of my face. I'm astonished. All I can say is, "That's a dildo."

"Actually, it's a vibrator," she says and turns the base. "Self-powered–like me."

"A vibrator? I can't believe my wife uses a vibrator...." I don't know if I should feel excited or extinct.

"Come on," she says, smiling and pulling me to her. "I want you." I want her too, and I can't remember when it's been so good. Fanny's gotten off twice, and I'm about to join her when she arches her hips, and I feel this distant vibration of something not quite touching me but touching me. I start to move faster and Fanny moans and I see one of the most satisfied smiles I've ever seen cross her face, and then I realize, if I'm inside her, then... "Oh, Jesus! You put it in T-H-E-R-E!" I stop moving for a second, then I start.

The next morning I go to the office late. My head's still spinning from the previous day's revelations about the Cuban gardener's grandson and the vibrator. I feel weak, nauseous, upset. I have no idea what's happening or why. I turn the doorknob. It's locked. Betty's been doing this lately for protection, even though we're on the thirtieth floor of a security high-rise. I unlock the door and look around. No lights, no Betty. She's not there, and she hasn't been. I check the messages on the machine. The fourth one is hers. "Not there today either, huh, Lenny. I'm going to stay home today, too. It's too nice to be in the office."

That's it. I close the door and go home. I can't finish anything without Betty anyhow. In the past several weeks she's changed vendors, switched software, and rearranged everything. I don't have a prayer.

"What about you?" Fanny says to me as soon as I open the door.

"What about me what?"

"Who else have you slept with?"

"Come on, Fanny. Not now."

"Why not now? I told you the truth, now you tell me...."

That's it. Now she has me. "Lenny be honest. That's all I want from you. Just be honest and tell me the truth." Every time she says this, I get creamed. The last time was a couple of weeks ago on a Sunday morning when I was reading the paper and she was finishing the puzzle and out of the blue she asked, "Who do you think is smarter, Lenny, me or you?" I don't say anything, just stare. I know better than this, I think. "Come on, Lenny, you can tell me. It won't kill you." I can feel myself starting to sweat. "Len–ny...." I shrug and begin to pray, "Yisgadal Vyiskadash..." The prayer for the dead. "Lenny, pleeeease...I *want* you to tell me the truth." So, "Ok," I say, "I'm a lawyer, I have three degrees to your two...." Before I even finish the sentence, her face is rock solid and icy cold. Just the way it is, they could put it right up there on Mt. Rushmore. She shakes her head at me in disbelief or sorrow or disappointment or regret–Who can tell?–then goes back to her puzzle and doesn't speak to me for the next three days.... So now what? She's Irish. If I tell her the truth about Sandy Waite, she'll never forgive and forget. I'll hear about it forever, for the rest of my life. And if I lie, she'll know it anyhow, and I'll have to stupidly gut it out....

"So who with?"

"Come on, Fanny...."

"Who?"

"No one."

"Len-ny?"

The phone rings. I go into my study to answer it. It's Betty. "You coming in tomorrow? I have something for you."

"Yes, I'm coming in tomorrow. There's work to be done. Are *you*?"

"I think so," she says, and hangs up.

I call Larry and tell him what's going on with Fanny. "What do you think, should I tell her or not?"

"Who cares, it doesn't matter. Whatever you do, you're fucked."

What the hell.... How much crazier can it get? I go back in and tell Fanny the truth.

"Was she pretty?" she wants to know.

"Yeah. I guess."

"Was she good, a good lover?"

"She was ok."

"Would I like her?"

"Jesus, I don't know, Fanny."

"What did she do?"

"My God, Fanny, what's the matter with you? What's come over you? I don't believe this. I didn't ask you anything about Juan or Fidel or whoever the Cuban was...."

"Jesús," she smiles. "What would you like to know?"

I decide to go back to the office. Whatever little I do there will be more than anything I accomplish here. I peek into the living room. Suzi's on the couch watching Oprah, but at least this time there's a blanket over her and she is holding a book in her lap, something by a Kathy Acker. From the cover, I can tell it's not good.

I go back upstairs to tell Fanny that I'm going back to the office.

"Shhhh," she says, "Oprah's on. She's interviewing women who've beaten up the men who've abused them."

I shake my head. "What about all the men who've been abused by women?" I mutter as I head down the stairs.

"Yesterday," Fanny yells. "Now it's our turn."

When I get to the office I'm surprised to find Betty there, busy typing. "Hi," I say, "glad you're here."

She ignores me, just nods and keeps typing.

"You look great. I like your hair." She does look great, new perm, new outfit, some kind of bolo tie.

"Thanks," she says, and keeps typing.

I go into my office and start to work. Ten minutes later Betty walks in without knocking and hands me a sheaf of papers. "I'll be out here," she says.

Now what! Can't a man even enjoy his work without interruptions? I look at what she's given me. Holy shit! It's a manifesto. An agreement. A contract! I read the first item:

> Mr. C shall treat Ms. S with all the respect professionally due her and her position; to wit, he shall not refer to her by her Christian name or any other names (such as, but not limited to, Dear, Honey, Sweetie, or Babe) but only by her surname unless officially, specifically, otherwise authorized by Ms. S to do so.

Oh, my God! Enough is enough already. When does this end? I read the whole thing over and am furious. I've had it. She even wants her own budget. I'm ready to fire her on the spot. I read it again, and well, it's not quite as bad as I thought. I read it a third time. Some of it is even helpful; some will make life easier for me. I read it over once more. It's actually pretty good. She's done a reasonable job of writing a contract. I feel proud. I pick up my pen and unscrew the cap and read it over one more time to be sure.

While I'm reading it, Betty walks in. She stands in the doorway waiting for me to finish and to decide what I'm going to do. I take my time and make her stand there. I hold my pen in the air and dangle it, then put it down on top of the contract, swivel my chair around and look out the window. My lunch is in my throat. Everything inside me is roaring *don't*: don't do it, don't sign, don't yield. Everything–bile, blood, marrow, sinew, synapses, chromosomes–ten thousand years of genetic history going back to Neanderthal Man, not to mention the guys at the club and the group.

I swivel my chair back around and look at Betty. She looks at me too, without doubt or abnegation: I see Suzi's glare, my mother-in-law's disappointment, Fanny's demand for the truth; even Beth and how she looked at me when she said she was leaving. I glare at Betty, angry at her for putting me in this position. She glares back. We're one on one, eyeball to eyeball, the issue between us is power. I am absolutely resolute even though I know I've already lost.

DREAMERS OF DREAMS

He will be back today. That's what Kevin said.

–One week. A week from tonight. Next Sunday.

–You're sure?

–Yes, I'm sure.

–And we'll spend the week together?

–Yes.

–The whole week?

–Every day. All day, until you have to go to work, and I'll meet you here on your evening break too, but I have to help my father train the new guy on the graveyard shift, remember?

–I remember.

–I'll be gone three months. Then after Basic I get a leave. Maybe you can fly for your Thanksgiving break and...

–Shhh. Not now. No more now. Hold me.

That was a week ago. Last Sunday. Nancy is sure of it. Today is Sunday, isn't it? It has to be. They're having beef for dinner. Beef is Sunday's dinner. Unless it's a holiday. Is it a holiday? Labor Day, maybe. Or someone's birthday. She looks around the dining room. No balloons or party hats. Nobody has wine at their table. But there are flowers. Maybe it is a holiday. Doesn't mean it's not Sunday, though. Holidays can be on Sundays. Easter is on Sunday. "Is this Sunday?"

Mildred Parks and Bea Fowler look at each other. They have come to expect these questions, but they still haven't gotten used to them. Sometimes they ignore her. Other times, to humor her, they respond.

"Well, is it?"

"Yes, Nancy, today is Sunday, August the twenty-eighth."

"All day," adds Mildred Parks.

Gleefully, Nancy returns to her food, sloshing the peas through the gravy.

"Will you be joining us this evening, Nancy? We're going to have music at eight."

"No, I don't think so." She pats her mouth with her napkin, signaling to the others that she is finished. "Not tonight. I'm too tired. Good night."

"Look how weak she is," she hears. "How unhappy...the way she dresses and acts!" Nancy ignores the comments. Pretending not to hear has allowed her to do what she wants all her life.

The walk back to her room has tired her. Nancy sits on her bed to rest, then begins with her preparations. She always starts with the table. She moves that first because it takes the longest and because she has most of her strength when she begins. It is how she has tackled everything in her life: hardest first. That way the important things get done.

Slowly, carefully, using the table as a walker, she moves it, inch by inch, across the worn and nubby rug. "Lift. Step. Stop," she chants to herself, pacing her movements, working her way closer to the window, refusing to look up until she arrives. "Lift. Step. Stop." She can hardly believe how she used to wile away her evenings at the Home playing bridge or listening to Caruso. At least now she has a purpose, something she always had before she came here. "Lift. Step. Stop." What does she care if the other ladies talk? Let them. Indeed, she rather enjoys it. It provides her with an identity all her own. "Lift.

Step. Stop." Her arms are getting tired. Her pace slower. Thank God the room is so small, no more than twelve feet wide. One more of life's little surprises. When she first moved in she despised the room's narrow confines and secluded ground-floor back-corner location, and now, well, now she appreciates the size of the Home–for the secrets it allows–and her room for its smallness and isolation. Even so, it often takes her five minutes or more just to move that beat-up tv table. Imagine! Five minutes to move a table nine or ten tiny feet. "Lift...Step...Stop." It's amazing how weak she's become. She has to remind herself: in her life she's accomplished things, even mountain-climbed. She had once been an adventurous woman, a woman to be reckoned with, which was why she married so late. And now? Now just moving a worn-out tv dinner table causes her heart to pound. She plops the table down in front of the window.

Exhausted, she drags herself back to her bed and collapses. She needs to recapture her strength. Her breathing is rapid and short. She counts, "One...two...three," as the exercise teacher has taught her, "four...five...six," and her breathing becomes slower and deeper. At eighty-seven, a second for every year, all of which seem to have gone just as fast, she sits up. Facing her is a photograph of herself when she was twenty. "It's like looking at another person in another life," she once told Maud. "I can hardly believe it was me." Maud laughed her horsey country laugh with clicking teeth. "It still is, Nancy-honey, it still is. That little girl's in you somewheres." Whenever she looks at that picture now, she always thinks of Maud. Easily she could forget their quarrels over Roosevelt and Hoover and their late-night, penny-ante gambling in which Maud never ceased trying to cheat, but for that one comment, that kindness. As long as she lives, she will think fondly of Maud. Once again, today, Nancy misses her used-to-be next-door neighbor. Maud, in her funny Arkansas, country-bumpkin conservative way, would understand exactly what she is doing. "It's just life, Nancy-honey," she'd say. "Just life.

Kick off your shoes an' 'preciate. Lord knows we ain't got much longer. So kick off your shoes an' 'preciate...." Nancy wishes Maud was still there to appreciate....

But she has no more time to dawdle. She still has plenty to do. Holding onto her cane, she stands and balances herself, feeling wobbly. Her muscles have tightened from resting. What a life! From sitting and relaxing, she stiffens up like a board, and from movement and exertion, she tires. Hobbling, she heads toward the bureau, counting her steps as she takes them. "One, two, three, four." She knows it's nine. It's always nine. But it keeps her mind on walking. If she thinks of anything else, she could fall.... Made it. She grasps the top of the bureau for balance with her right hand and switches her cane to her left. Then, cautiously, with difficulty, feeling the muscles pull in her thighs, her lower back, she jerkily bends at the knees, totters, steadies herself, opens the middle drawer, and locates the napkins she wants—the linen ones she bought in Ireland. She removes three from the drawer, tucks them under her arm, straightens herself out, and carries them back to the table. "One, two, three...."

Six more times she makes this journey: for sherry, cheese, crackers, a glass, a plate, and a bowl. Each time she counts her steps. One step after the other. Nothing in life prepares you for getting old. Nothing.

Nancy unfolds two napkins and wipes away the wrinkles—if only it were so easy, if only it were—and lays them across the table. She walks the circumference of the table, gripping the edge for support, tugging at the napkins, a push here, a pull there, making certain they are evenly spread. Then she puts down the plate, the bowl and the glass. She is tired. She can feel it taking charge of her body: her fingers are swollen and itchy; the nerves in her back are throbbing. Slow down, she tells herself, slow down, then laughs. Any slower and she wouldn't be moving at all!

"That will come soon enough," she mutters. "Sooner than soon enough." She unwraps the cheese and centers it on the plate and arranges the crackers in the bowl. She picks up a pewter bud vase with a white chrysanthemum—her favorite flower—which she picked that afternoon, and slides it to a corner of the table. Then shakily—from all her exertion, not Parkinson's, no, not Parkinson's—she pours the sherry from a half-full bottle into her crystal decanter. With the napkin she saved for herself, she wipes the drops that have spilled.

She is weary now, filled with fatigue. The throbbing in her back has spread to her feet. Her shoulders feel weighted with lead. Still, she refuses to quit. If she does, she knows she'll never get started again. Compelling herself forward, Nancy continues. She dusts away cracker crumbs, rubs at the wine stain, straightens everything. Everything must be perfect. She looks at the window to make sure it is open, stares for a moment at the empty gazebo, then reaches, stretches, strains, hauls the curtains shut, and eases herself onto her rocker. The pulse in her neck is exploding. Her body is a house on fire. "One, two, three," she counts to relax, "four, five, six...." She stops at eighty-two, the age at which she was widowed. Without looking in a mirror—she hardly ever uses a mirror anymore—she lipsticks her lips, rouges her cheeks, powders her nose, slips a handkerchief up her sleeve. Finished, she pours a glass of sherry and sips. She breaks a piece of cheese and nibbles. Then she reaches up behind her and dims the overhead light. From the bookcase to her left she retrieves the book she wants, her companion for all these years.

The book, *A Golden Treasury of Great Poems*, cracks open to the place it always does, to Arthur O'Shaughnessey's "Ode." From memory, Nancy speaks the opening lines. "We are the music-makers/ And we are the dreamers of dreams." In all of the book, these are her favorite words. Silently, for herself, she repeats them. Then turning the page, she reads the last two lines aloud. "For each age is a dream that is dying/ Or one that is coming to birth." Those were Maud's favorites. Nancy smiles. Right there was the difference between them.

She recalls the first time she read them to Maud. "Nancy-honey, that's beau-ti-ful. Wisht I'da done more readin'. Wisht I'da 'sperienced some of those things. Read it agin, Nancy-honey. Read it agin." For Maud, Nancy reads it again. Then she stands and refills her glass. She sips, takes a cracker, and chews. Inside it is getting dark. Outside, it is darker still. She looks at her clock. It's 8:35. Kevin must have lost track of the time. She empties her glass, pours another and sips. The sherry tastes like honey in her mouth. She takes another piece of cheese, places it on a cracker, and nibbles and sips some more. Turning the pages, she reads one poem by Byron, another by Shelley, and a third by Keats: the Romantics, with their restrained, intellectualized passion. After each poem she pauses, looks at her clock, and nibbles and sips, nibbles and sips....

Nancy's head jerks. She can feel it bob. Groggily she opens her eyes. Half-awake, half-asleep, she is conscious of the stitch in her neck. Closing her eyes, she presses the area that hurts. Then, in panic–remembering her plans–she stares at the clock: 11:42. No! Rubbing the sleep from her eyes, she looks again: 11:43. No. No. No. She wouldn't have slept through their visit. Couldn't. Their talking would have awakened her. She's sure of it. She's not that sound a sleeper. The slightest noise is able to wake her–a toilet flushing, a television too loud, footsteps on the thickly carpeted hallway. So what happened? It has to be something. She is certain he said Sunday. Next Sunday. Maybe his plane was delayed. That could be it. Or something unexpected came up: an illness, a family problem, an emergency. Despondent, she pushes herself forward. A jolt like an electric shock shoots through her body. Tomorrow, she tells herself, tomorrow. They have to come tomorrow. Kevin will only be here for another week. That's what he said: "One week." Holding tight to her cane, she stands, picks up the bowl, and begins to recircle the table. "One, two, three...."

❖

Nancy wakes up late, tired, and stays in bed. She feels foolish, waiting on people who fail to show up. It's rude, she thinks, then reminds herself it is she who is transgressing, not they. Still, she is upset. In the hallway she hears footsteps—Mrs. Wallace. She can tell by the speed of the steps. She's here to complain about breakfast. Nancy shuts her eyes and waits.

"Nancy?"

Eyes open.

"Are you feeling all right?"

Eyes shut. She hates it when people just barge into her room—Mrs. Wallace, the nurses, Stephanie, anyone. To her way of thinking it is rude. It certainly doesn't deserve a response.

"Nancy?"

Eyes open.

"I was concerned."

"No need."

"You missed breakfast again." Eyes shut. "I thought all that ended last week. We're not going to start *that* again, are we?"

Eyes open.

"Nan-cy!" She sits on the edge of the bed. "It's time to get up now, Nancy."

"I don't want to."

"The hairdresser is waiting."

"Today?"

Mrs. Wallace stands up. "All right then, I'll tell him you're coming." She opens the door to leave.

"Mrs. Wallace?" Nancy sounds contrite.

"Yes." She is expecting an explanation—or maybe even an apology. "What is it, Nancy?"

"Don't let him do Mildred Parks first. She always takes too much time."

Nancy feels better after having her hair done. But when she thinks of their absence, she's depressed. At lunch, she sits solemnly and eats.

"Nancy, your hair looks lovely."

She says nothing.

"Is that a new dress? You look so pretty today."

Nancy smiles. Of course it's not a new dress. They know it's not a new dress. She hates it when they act solicitous towards her, as if they are better than she.

"Are you going out?"

Nancy nods. "Stephanie is taking me shopping." That's all she intends to say. She knows she is being impolite, but she doesn't care. She is tired of all their small talk. When Maud was there she laughed.

For a while they all sit quietly. The ladies all around them buzzing. Finally, to break the awkwardness of the situation, Bea Fowler asks, "Where will you be going?"

"To the market."

Bea looks over at Mildred Parks. Nancy sees them exchange glances. She thinks they are going to ask her to pick up something for them. If so, she'll be caught in her lie. No, she smiles, she'll tell them she forgot. That, she knows, they'll believe.

"Are you expecting company?"

Nancy blanches, goes cold and lowers her eyes to her hands. Her fingers feel just like icicles. "No, just Stephanie. That's all. I like to have something to eat in my room. You know how poor the food is here. Why, I can't even eat the breakfasts."

In unison, Mildred and Bea resume their meals as Nancy stands and excuses herself. "I have to go call Stephanie and see what time she is coming."

"Hello, Stephanie."

"Hi, Mom."

"What time are you coming today?"

"Today? I hadn't planned on coming today. Who said anything about today?"

"You said you'd see me in a few days."

"I was planning on visiting tomorrow."

"I may be busy. Why not today?"

"I can't today. I have to take Jason to the dentist."

"Oh."

"I can come on Wednesday if tomorrow's not good for you."

"Tomorrow's fine."

"But I thought...you said...."

"See you tomorrow. Bye."

The remainder of the day Nancy frets. She busies herself in her room. She dusts her bureau and arranges the photos on her nightstand, pushing Stephanie's to the rear, out of sight. Through the window she sees Mildred and Bea sitting in the gazebo, the two of them chattering away like a couple of magpies. Nancy sits on her rocker and listens.

"Isn't it lovely?"

"Yes."

"And so private."

"Nancy?" It's Mrs. Wallace. "Are you asleep, Nancy?"

"How could anyone sleep around here." She is talking to the window.

"People making noise in the garden." She turns to face Mrs. Wallace. "There's never any privacy or peace."

Mrs. Wallace laughs and sits down on the edge of her bed. "I've been worried about you, Nancy. We all have."

"No need."

"Are you feeling all right?"

"Fine."

"You seem so angry."

"I'm not. Just old."

Mrs. Wallace shakes her head and stands. Nancy returns her gaze to the gazebo. She hears the doorknob turn. "Would you like to go out and sit in the sun before it rains?"

"No. I don't want to do anything. I just want to sit here and rot."

At six-fifteen Nancy enters the dining room. Mildred and Bea are there, still talking. When Nancy sits down, they clam up. She's sure they have been talking about her.

"Did you go shopping today, Nancy? We didn't see Stephanie's car." Mildred nods her affirmation to Bea.

"Jason had an accident. Stephanie had to take him to the doctor."

"Is he all right?"

"Is it serious?"

"Everything is fine." Nancy smiles. "A tiny cut. Stephanie will come tomorrow. Would you like me to get you something from the store?"

Bea smiles back. "Thank you. But my Joanie will take me on Thursday."

"No," says Mildred Parks.

Before the dessert arrives, Nancy stands up to leave.

"Will you be coming back for the music? They're going to be doing Mozart tonight."

"No. I'm tired."

"But he's your favorite."

"If I want to I can listen from my room."

By seven forty-five the curtains are drawn shut and the table is in place and laid out. Nancy is sitting and waiting, agitated, feeling foolish and trying to remain calm. The pain in her back is troubling, but outweighed by the pain in her heart. She counts: "One, two, three, four..." and stops at eighty-three, her age when she entered the Home. That's what her exercise teacher told her. "Think of a number that has significance to your life and count to it. Afterwards, you'll be calm and more at ease." Nancy counts to thirty-six, her age when Stephanie was born. She is trying to do everything right. If she does it right, she thinks, they will come. If she does it the way she usually does, everything will work out fine. She looks at the table. There's no flower. Her little rebellion. After last night they don't deserve a flower. No, not after making her wait. Still, it bothers her. If she doesn't do it right, they may not come. She chastises herself. Either they will come or they won't. The flower has nothing to do with it. She looks at her clock. It's 7:48. She has finished setting up earlier than usual. She breaks a piece of cheese and pours herself a glass of sherry—and she wishes she had gotten a flower.

At 7:55 she begins to read the "Ode." To pass the time, she reads it aloud. After repeating it twice, she does the same with three poems by the Romantics. In between each reading she sips at her glass of sherry, looks at the clock, stares at the window, and tells herself it's still early. It's only 8:15...just 8:25...barely 8:45.... She counts to thirty, the age at which she married Will. She drinks some sherry and tells herself she will only wait up until nine. At 9:00 she gives them until 9:15. At 9:15 she gives them until 9:30. After that, she refuses to look at the clock. She flips the pages of her book and settles on

Edgar Allen Poe. She begins reading "Annabelle Lee," first to herself to get the rhythm, then softly, quietly, out loud. She turns the page to "The Raven." When finished, she checks the time: 10:12. She feels like a fool. An old fool. Once more, she's waited for nothing. She looks at her neatly set table and shudders. Then, more with anger than strength, she pushes herself up and begins to replace her things. "One, two, three...." She stops and stares at the window. Her entire body is shaking from the inside out. The effort of standing is painful. Still, she stands and stares. Then she continues her journey. "Seven, eight, nine...." She walks to the windowsill, pulls back the curtain, and looks out at the empty gazebo. Everything is quiet and black. Wiping a tear from her cheek, she continues her gaze. Then, from somewhere deep inside, deeper than breath and deeper than pain, she mutters: "Nevermore." Released, it feels good. So she says it again, louder. "Nevermore... Nevermore. Nevermore. Nevermore."

"Mother...Mother, wake up."

"I don't want any breakfast."

"Mother, it's me, Stephanie."

Nancy turns and raises her head. "Oh."

"Come on, get up."

"I don't want to go shopping. I don't need to."

Stephanie laughs. Nancy scowls: why does everyone laugh when she's upset? "Come on. I've made reservations at your favorite place for lunch."

"I'm not hungry."

"Well, you should be. Mrs. Wallace tells me you've been missing your breakfasts again."

Nancy props herself up on her pillow.

"And I just saw Mrs. Parks. She told me you told her Jason had an accident yesterday."

"You said you were taking him to the doctor."

"To the dentist. For a filling. That's all."

"Oh." She flops back down.

"Mother, are you ok?"

"Fine."

"Maybe I should call the doctor."

"I said I was fine. Perfect. I'm just old, that's all. An old fool."

Stephanie walks over to the window. "The garden is beautiful this time of year." She turns around. Nancy sees that she notices her picture. Usually it is right up front. Now it is hidden by the others. Stephanie takes in the room. Her eyes settle on the empty sherry bottle in the wastebasket.

"I'm coming. I'm coming. Give me time. When you get to be my age, you'll want all the time you can get."

Stephanie brings Nancy her cane, then helps her into the bathroom. Nancy knows she is rummaging through her room, trying to read the signs. "Bring me my red dress, will you?"

Stephanie hands her her dress and leaves the door open. Nancy knows Stephanie's afraid she might fall. She closes the door. Stephanie clears her throat. "I spoke to Maud yesterday."

"Who?"

"Maud. You remember Maud, don't you?"

"Of course I remember Maud. I'm old, I said, not senile."

"She says to say hello. We could visit her if you like. She's at Beachview Convalescent."

Nancy sticks her head out the door. "No. I don't like. I don't want to go to one of those places. I'll be there soon enough."

Back in her room, tired from lunch and shopping and Stephanie's pestering questions, Nancy lies down and takes a nap. When she awakens, she notices her position and stretches. For fifty-three years she has slept on the left side of the bed, curved like an S hook, her right arm hugging Will's pillow. Fifty-three years. In the beginning she couldn't get used to sleeping with him, and now she can't get used to not. She pushes herself up and sits there, staring at the clock. She refuses to look at his picture, at his smiling, successful, forty-year-old face. If she sees it, she will think of their past—their good times, her youth, their happiness—and she will become angry with him again, angry for dying so foolishly, trying to save a dog, and for making her spend her last days alone, alone in this place to rot.

She stands and straightens her dress, then begins to unpack the groceries. She sets the two apples she bought, a Golden Delicious and a McIntosh, on the windowsill. She puts the sherry, crackers, cheese, and jam in the closet. Then she closes and locks her door and carefully makes her way to the dining room. For a change, Nancy tells herself, she'll be the first person there. But mostly, she knows, she wants to get out of her room.

"Look," she hears Mildred exclaim to Bea, "it's Nancy."

"Nancy, it's so nice to see you. And *so* early!"

Nancy smiles.

"And for fish too!"

Nancy smiles wider.

During the meal she eats very quietly. She feels like just another of the sixty-five women having dinner. Once she says something about the weather. Later, she praises the garden and how pretty the rose bushes look by the gazebo. Mostly, though, she ignores her table-mates, occasionally looking up to smile and nod at their stupidities. Then, in a lull, waiting until their mouths are filled with dessert, Nancy asks, "Is there a movie tonight?"

Bea bobs her head up and down. Mildred chews faster and swallows hard. "Certainly, Nancy." She dabs at her mouth with her napkin. "Today's Tuesday, isn't it!"

"What time?"

"Why, at eight. It's always at eight. On Tuesdays. You remember that, don't you Nancy?"

Nancy dabs at her mouth, mimicking Mildred Parks. "Excuse me," she says, as she pushes herself away from the table. With effort and as much dignity as she can conjure, she turns and shuffles off into the living room and settles herself at the card table. For the next hour she watches the clock and worries about not being in her room should they come tonight, certain they won't, playing solitaire. Finally, at 7:50 the other ladies begin to arrive. Nancy sees Mildred and Bea enter together. They see her too, and as quickly as possible—silently, in unison—they move toward the couch farthest away from where she is sitting. For a second or two Nancy stares at them and at the other ladies who have entered, and she wishes that Maud was still there. Maud and Will and Kevin and Becky and everyone else who has left her....

12:15. She's slept through lunch as well as breakfast. She rolls over. At 12:45 she sits up, feels dizzy and weak, and lies back down. She is hungry—knows she should eat—but doesn't feel like going to the closet for crackers and cheese or jam. She wants an apple. She reaches for her cane, stands jerkily, waits to get her balance, and slowly, unevenly, practically hearing her bones, moves herself over to the window. It's the McIntosh she wants, made warm and sweet by the sun. Already she can taste its juice, feel its red, waxy skin, her first bite. At the window she stops and rests, inhales and exhales several times to catch her breath, relaxes, and pulls aside the curtains, anticipating, and sees only the Golden Delicious. The McIntosh is gone, probably rolled onto the floor. She places one hand on the windowsill to steady herself, keeps the other hand gripping her cane, and bends at the waist, half crouches, and searches the floor for her apple. It's not there. She straightens herself up, puts both hands on the windowsill and looks out into the bushes beneath her window. It's not there either–her mouth has gone from wet to dry. It's gone. They took it! Kevin and Becky! They came and took her apple. They came while she was at the movie and stole it. They sneaked up and stole her apple.

"Nancy!"

Mrs. Wallace! Nancy turns to face her, her whole body sagging, held up by the tip of her cane.

"Nancy, you missed....what's wrong?"

"They took my apple."

"Who? Who took your apple? The nurse?"

Nancy shakes her head no. "They did...." and is sorry as soon as she says it.

"Who? Who's they?"

"Thieves."

"Oh?"

"They did! *Look*!" She points with her cane. "I had two apples yesterday, and now I have only one. Ask Stephanie!"

Mrs. Wallace walks to the window and peers out. "There it is, Nancy, the core. You must have eaten it and dropped it yourself...."

"I did not. I should know. It was stolen."

"By thieves?"

Nancy nods.

"Do you know them–these thieves? Have you ever seen them before?"

Nancy shrugs.

"Maybe we're a little confused today, Nancy. That can happen to us, you know, when we don't eat our..."

"I'm not confused." She straightens herself up. "They sneaked up here last night and stole it. They knew I was at the movie and took it. They're thieves."

"Now, Nancy..."—Nancy trembles—"really, now Nancy, why would anybody want...I'll be right back."

Mrs. Wallace returns with the nurse. "Now, Nancy, Mrs. Jackson is going to give you a little something to calm you."

"I don't want anything...." She raises her cane, "I don't need it..." holds the cane in the air, "I won't have it...." and bangs the cane on the floor. "They're thieves." She bangs it again. "Ask Stephanie."

"Now, Nancy...."

Outside, everything is pitch black, the moon and stars hidden and blocked by the Home. Inside, her nightlight is on. Nancy turns. Beside her bed is a cold plate. She ignores it, hugs, then punches Will's pillow, and tries to go back to sleep but can't. Her mind is more active than her body. Eyes open, she lies in bed. Years ago this was her favorite time. She would wake up early, before the sun, read the paper, maybe write a letter, make coffee and plans, and have breakfast ready for Will and Stephanie when they woke up. The quiet of the house then was comforting, reassuring, providing time and pleasure in her life. But now—as on this morning—she either stays in bed or sleeps late, having nothing better to do. Staring out the window, through the still-parted curtains, she waits for the new day's light.

A thunder crack startles Nancy out of her sleep. She opens her eyes and sees that the cold plate is gone. Sleep and eat and sleep. Full circle. Like a baby again. This is what her life has become. She tucks the covers tightly around her, listens to the summer rain pelt her window and waits for more thunder to come.

All day, through thunder and lightning and rain, Nancy remains in bed. When the telephone rings—it's probably Stephanie—she doesn't answer it. And when Mrs. Wallace comes into her room without knocking, Nancy pretends she's asleep.

"Nancy...."

She squeezes her eyes tightly shut.

"Nancy?"

The voice is a little louder, nearer. Nancy's heart flutters. A cold hand touches her forehead. She tenses, then relaxes, as Mrs. Wallace moves away. Nancy listens, counts the steps, as Mrs. Wallace walks towards the door and stops: she is staring, staring at this foolish old shell called Nancy. Nancy waits. The door opens. Mrs. Wallace hesitates, lingers, then says, "Poor Nancy," and closes the door behind her.

Nancy rolls back over, lays her head on Will's pillow, and stares out the window at the rain.

When a heavyset aide barges into her room and thumps down a tray on the night table, Nancy pushes herself up and glares. The aide glowers back, then turns away in disgust, grabs at the doorknob and says, "Better be done when I get back, hear!" and shuts the door sharply.

Nancy sits up. On the tray is a chicken potpie, corn bread, salad, a brownie, and a pot of tea. She breaks apart the potpie, nibbles at a piece of bread, a chunk of chicken, a few slivers of potato, and leaves everything else untouched. She is too upset to be hungry. For a minute or two she sits there, aimless. Then she snatches her cane, picks up the plate, and, hunched over and stiff, carries it into the bathroom and empties it all into the toilet. Retracing her steps, she does the same with the brownie, the bread, and the tea. Then she pushes the emergency intercom button that is set in the wall beside her bed. "All done," she announces. "Come and take it away."

Twenty minutes later the aide returns for the tray. Nancy says nothing as she sits in her rocker and rocks, and when the aide smiles, seeing that the plates are empty, and says, "Now, wasn't that good?"

Nancy smiles back and says, "Yes, yes it was. *Very* good."

Nancy hears voices. She turns towards the window–silence. She looks at her clock. It's 7:16. More voices, louder. She looks at the window again, then at the door. It's the other ladies in the hallway, returning to their rooms after dinner–talking, laughing, together. She turns on her television but doesn't listen or watch. She picks up her book but doesn't read. Exhausted. Her mind is as worn as her body. She rocks, fitfully dozes, rocks and dozes some more, as the television newsman drones on, and her book casually slips from the crease in her lap to the rug....

A noise. Outside. In the bushes. Nancy perks, listens, hears nothing. She bends over–feels a jolt in her back–picks up her book, and reads, "We are the music-makers/ And we are the dreamers of dreams." Another noise. A voice? The breeze? She stands. Her legs ache. She half-steps her way to the window, looks out at the sunset–at the gold and magenta sky, the roses, tulips, peonies, and lilies in full bloom–and sees nothing but the empty gazebo. For several minutes she remains there, lamenting her age, her place, her condition. Then she pulls the curtains shut, turns around, and looks at her room–the room she first disliked, then liked, now despises–and hobbles her way back to her rocker. On the television, a preacher promises deliverance to those who truly believe.

–C'mon. (Kevin?) –She's there. (Yes, it's Becky.) –Nobody's there, c'mon. (They've come back.) –I know she's there. She'll hear us. (Nancy leans forward.) –She's asleep. They're all asleep. Look. The lights are all out. (Thank God she didn't turn on her light.)–Her's isn't. (The television!) –It's a safety light. That's all. Or she fell asleep with her tv on." (Nancy turns down the volume, afraid to turn off the set.) –C'mon, Becky. C'mon. (Nancy waits, expectant, gripping the arms of her rocker.) –No. (She stands.) –We'll get caught. (Hesitates.) –Tomorrow. I promise. Not tonight. (Takes a step and trips over the leg of her rocker.)

She pulls herself up on all fours and crawls to the window and waits. She counts to fifty–a number that means nothing to her at all –reaches for the windowsill, hauls herself up to the window, opens the curtains, and looks out. Nothing. No one. They disappeared like ghosts. Nancy stands there, her ankle and knuckles pounding, staring, hoping to catch a glimpse of Kevin and Becky–to see what they look like, or at least some proof of their presence. She looks to her left, her right, straight ahead, and there on the path in the light, she sees the core of an apple. Her other apple! She had forgotten it. They came again last night while she was sleeping. Drugged. Two nights in a row they came back, and each time she missed their visit. The first night she went to the movie. The second night she was sleeping, drugged. Two nights in a row. No, three. Three nights in a row. Three nights counting tonight. When they come back tomorrow–Becky said they would. "Tomorrow," she said. "I promise...."

Her last chance. Their last day. Today she will do everything right: go to all her meals, dress properly, straighten her room, even play bingo in the afternoon; everything will be done by the book. She stands and winces and falters. She forgot about her ankle, which is now swollen and blue. For a moment she remains there, stationary, allowing her body to acclimate itself to this new pain. Then she limps to her closet, takes down her new dress–the one she's never worn, the one Stephanie gave her for her last birthday–and puts it on. Sitting on her bed, she pulls on a pair of stockings and examines herself in the mirror. She looks good. Good for an eighty-seven-year-old.

Everything matches and fits, and the stockings cover the blue of her bruise.

By eleven o'clock she has eaten breakfast, picked up everything from her floor, packed away her clothes, and emptied her wastebasket into the hall incinerator. Worn out, she lies down to rest. Facing her is Stephanie's photograph. She reaches up, pushes it to the front, then picks up the phone and calls her.

"Stephanie, dear, I need some apples."

"Today? Does it have to be today? I'm awful busy."

"I need them for my digestion."

"Oh?"

"The nurse said they're good for my system."

"Ok, Mother."

"By dinnertime."

"Ok, Mother. But I can't stay."

"That's fine, dear. Just fine. Goodbye."

During lunch Nancy is on her best behavior. She eats without making a mess, asks Bea about her Joanie, tells Mildred how nice she looks, and accepts their compliments about her new dress. She even makes plans to join them later for bingo. All in all, considering their banality, lunch proves to be one of their better encounters. Nancy pats her mouth and stands. "Would you excuse me, please? I'm going out to sit in the garden. I'll see you at two-thirty for bingo." She picks up her cane and turns. "Oh," she turns back, "Stephanie will be bringing me some apples later. Would you care for any?"

"Yes. Thank you, Nancy," says Bea.

"I wish I could," says Mildred, tapping her teeth with her fingers. "It's been years since I've been able to eat an apple."

Nancy smiles and walks away—trying hard not to favor her ankle visibly. She stops at the front door, counts to seventy-two, her age when Jason was born, and looks through the glass at the sky. It is clear, almost cloudless, rich blue and sunny. She opens the door, half-steps her way down the ramp, and makes her way over to the gazebo, walking past the first bench, the second, and the third and folds herself down on the fourth. Maud's bench. The bench Maud sat on whenever the weather was friendly. "Seems friendly out," Maud would say. "Think I'll go sit with the roses." Mr. Jorgensen, the gardener, waves. Nancy waves back. The flowers, all plush in their reds, yellows, blues, and white, move effortlessly, like dancers in the air. The air, clean and crisp, smells like honey. Even the fertilizer is pleasant to Nancy's nostrils, alive. She closes her eyes, breathes deeply, letting the warmth from the sun warm her and the breeze brush over her skin. Already she can taste her triumph, her moment of glory—her capture of Kevin and Becky.

At two-thirty she is back in the dining room playing bingo. By four-thirty she has won three dollars and fifty cents. "I knew it," she gloats to Mrs. Wallace in the hallway, "*Today* is my lucky day." She opens her door: on her bureau is a huge bouquet of white chrysanthemums from Mr. Jorgensen; on her bed are a half dozen apples. Nancy picks up each apple—examines it, squeezes it, smells it—and selects the best one, a pippin, for her plan. She limps to the window, places the apple on the sill, and stands there appreciating her handiwork. Then, even though her stomach is much too excited for her to eat, she drops the remaining apples into a bag and hobbles down the hall to the dining room.

Nancy is sitting in her rocker, relieved. She made it with no mistakes. The whole day according to plan. For a while there—at dinner—she thought she'd lose it: Bea going on and on about the apples, how nice they looked, how juicy they seemed, how apples, along with all other fruits and vegetables, are not what they used to be; and

Mildred discussing her teeth: her old ones, her new ones, her bridge, her gums. Interminable. But Nancy waited, forced herself not to be brusque, to smile and nod, pretending to listen and care. And she made it. Now all she has to do is wait.

She picks up her book and lays it on her lap but is too preoccupied to read. She doesn't drink any sherry—that way she won't get drowsy. The television is off so there won't be any noise. Her table isn't set because she doesn't want the nurse to see it when she calls her in to catch them. Only her night-light is on. She is listening for the slightest sound: a moving bush, a crunched twig, a whisper.... There! She stops rocking...leans forward...concentrates. Nothing. She waits to be sure, resumes rocking and waits. 8:20...8:25...8:40... a voice? No, it's coming from the hallway. One of the ladies. Three more times she thinks she hears them. Each time proves to be nothing: a breeze, a cat, someone moving some furniture upstairs. She thumbs through the pages of her book, looks at the clock, which she had been trying to avoid, and sees that it's 9:28. For the first time that day, Nancy begins to doubt that they'll come, that Becky changed her mind, that once again, she's...a voice! Outside. She leans forward. Something brushes against her window. She holds her breath, listens...nothing. She leans back. A leaf crunches. She leans forward—heart pounding, breathing stilled—tightly holding onto the book in her lap, certain that someone is out there. —Don't be upset. (It's Kevin.) —I'm not. (Becky sounds sad.) —You sure? —Yes, I just miss you already, that's all.

For a long time they don't speak. Nancy sits back, slowly rocking. She is waiting for Becky—she is sure it is Becky—to see her apple and take it. Then she will call the nurse.

—Becky?

—Hmmmm.

—What are you thinking?

Nancy stops rocking, leans forward. The book on her lap thumps to the floor.

—What's that!

—Nothing.

—Yes, it is. She's in there.

—No. Listen. Nobody's there.

Quietly, deliberately—afraid that they might suddenly leave—Nancy stands, steps over her book, and very, very slowly makes her way over to her bed. She puts her hands on the mattress and gradually, incrementally, sits, hoping the box springs won't creak. One push and the nurse will be there. She lifts her arm, places her finger on the emergency button, slightly depresses it—and hesitates. She doesn't want to do it too soon.

—She's asleep.

—She's not, but I don't care. Tonight's our last night anyhow.

—Shhh. No more now. Tell me what you were thinking.

—It's silly.

—Tell me anyhow.

—I was thinking about being old. Do you ever think about that? Being old?

Kevin laughs. —I *am* old. Almost twenty-one. I'm three years older than you.

—No, I mean old, old. Like...like the lady who lives in that room.

The bushes rustle. Nancy imagines Kevin putting his arm around Becky and hugging her, the way Will used to do with her when she was upset. She leans forward, and together she and Becky wait....

—Sometimes I think about it. Sure. But when I do, I think about you. About us. I see the two of us, retired, all gray and hunched over and wrinkled, walking along hand in hand, talking about the kids and the grandchildren, complaining about how they're being brought up.

—Kevin, I love you.

—I love *you*. I always will. Forever. I swear.

Everything is quiet after that. Nancy sits perfectly still—her finger no longer on the button. She pictures them holding hands, maybe kissing, looking up at the moon and the stars, the same moon and stars she and Will sat under when they sneaked down to the river to be alone. There they would talk for hours: he telling her his plans to become a veterinarian; she telling him all the places she wanted to see. All those words and those dreams, so protected by their youth, so hopeful, so certain that they would never be old, that time and catastrophe would pass them by. All of that comes back to her, to Nancy, to Nona, as Will called her, as she sits there perfectly still.

—C'mon, Becky, I have to go help my father, and you have to get back to work.

—Wait a minute. I have to do something.

Nancy hears some paper crumbling...Kevin's laugh...the bushes rustling...and she wishes them well. Then, when she is certain that they have left, she hobbles to her window and draws back the curtains to look out. There, on the windowsill, on either side of her apple, sit two more. A McIntosh and a Golden Delicious. For several minutes Nancy stands there bathed in the light of the moon. Then she picks up the apples and holds them, rolling each one over her cheeks.

Mementos

I'm upstairs in the tv room peeking out the window watching my son play catch. He's playing with the next-door neighbor kids, Willie and Wendy, and he's not doing anything I taught him. He shies away from grounders. He doesn't get down. He doesn't charge the ball. He lets it eat him. He muffs one out of three, and those he does catch he snatches one-handed, off to the side. It worries me. He's playing it safe, laying back. He's a little bit chicken, a scaredy-cat: nothing at all like me. I continue to watch him, amazed yet again by his softness, his gentleness, what Vicki calls his Spirit—by which she means something other than guts or *cojones*. He bounces a throw to Willie and says, "I'm sorry." He misjudges a pop-up and giggles. And his outfit! A Dodger-blue hat that's too big for him, yellow designer sweats, orange wrist bands, and bright-red sneakers with multilayered patented soles and Velcro instead of laces. I shake my head. "At his age I was sharpening my spikes...!"

I turn around quickly. Vicki didn't hear me. She's still in the study doing some work. "At-his-age-you-lived-in-Brooklyn-for-God's-sake." I'm mimicking her. I have the rhythm down, but not the tone. When she says it, it sounds as if she's explaining creation. I sound like my father imitating his mother. "We-came-here-to-give-Evan-something-better...." I'm still doing Vicki, but I stop as I see Tom, our gay across-the-street neighbor, get out of a car and then reach back in and hug his date from the previous night good-bye. "See you," he calls out and waves. "Have a nice day."

I close my eyes and shudder. What am I doing here, I ask myself for the ten millionth time in six months, in Los Angeles. "Land of sproutheads, fruitcakes, and nuts." I open my eyes. Vicki's reflection is in the window. Already, before breakfast, I've blown it. "I don't know where that came from," I tell her. "I really don't."

"I do," she says as she picks up a towel and goes into the bathroom. "It's just what your father would say."

I remain at the window looking out. Vicki joins me when she finishes showering. She puts her arm around me, hooks her thumb under my belt through a belt loop, and tugs. "He's got it, doesn't he?" she says.

I put my arm around her and pull her close. She means the look. I have it, my brother Ricky has it, and so does my father and my father's father too. Generation after generation of Rossini men, narrow-shouldered, long-legged, lean-hipped, and angular-faced, with cavernous eyes and that famous Rossini mouth: full-lipped and toothy, torn between a grin and a bite.

"Everything but the paunch," I say, and I pat my belly as I say it. I don't really have a paunch, but Vicki likes to say I do, and I am anxious now to please her. She rubs it. "Three times and you can have what you want." I wink as I say this and Vicki laughs.

Then she looks up at me and asks, "What do *you* want, Stan?" and I'm stuck. I look out the window at Evan. He's lying on the grass looking up. What does he see, I wonder? What does *he* want? I should ask him, I know, but I'm afraid. I'm afraid he'll say something sweet like Vicki would say. At his age I wanted to be Willie Mays, Audie Murphy, John Wayne.

"So! What is it?" Vicki is squeezing me now almost as much as I'm squeezing her. My wish? My wish? My wish is that my son looked more like his mother and acted more like me. I look at Vicki. She's waiting, still smiling, expectant. There's no way on earth I can tell her. I say, "I hope the Giants beat the Dodgers again."

Vicki goes back to the bathroom. I stay at the window looking out, but it's no longer Evan I see. Dad's throwing me high hard ones and tricky grounders, and I'm scooting left, right, back, forward, snatching anything and everything he tosses. He throws harder and harder, zingers and fireballs, on the line, frozen rope. "Come on," he yells, "let's just see what you've got." I show him. No matter how much my hand hurts I won't stop. God, I was pretty to see. Even Dad said so. "Great hands," he'd say. "If only the kid could hit."

I'm drinking my third cup of coffee, waiting for Vicki and reading over yesterday's box scores. I've already got breakfast planned—my special-for-Vicki vegetarian omelette smothered in Rossini-family secret sauce. I hear her come down the stairs. She sticks her head in the doorway. "I'm going out to breakfast with my mom." I lower the paper and look at her. I can't see all of her, but I can tell she's dressed up and spiffy-looking. "Say hello," I say, and grin. Then I hide behind the paper and stick out my tongue and make all kinds of animal-monster faces. I know she's going to see her mom to commiserate. Her mom thinks I'm a jerk. Vicki thinks her mom is a bobblehead. The only time they get together like this is when they both agree about me.

I follow her out to her car and open the door and hold it for her. She stands there in front of the door, not moving, her arms crossed and folded across her chest. I don't say anything. I just wait. Finally she unfolds her arms and runs her fingers through her hair, and I smile. This is what I've been waiting for. This is what she does when she's speechless and amazed, when she finds herself wondering again how in God's vast Kingdom she wound up married to me. I put my arms around her and kiss her, Eskimo-style, rubbing my nose on hers. "Stop it," she says, pushing me away, trying to suppress a smile. "I'll be back in the afternoon."

"What am I supposed to do?"

"I don't know, Stan. Build a battleship. Start a war. Teach Evan to be a real man."

"I might," I say. "I just might."

Vicki shakes her head and gets into her car. From across the street Tom waves to her as she drives away, then he waves to me and returns to his gardening. I watch for a moment as he works. At least once a week he and Vicki share gardening secrets about fertilizer, moisture, soil, seed, pruning, mulch, whatever. I couldn't care less. I'm just happy that Evan is twelve, old enough to weed and mow. Left to me, the place would become a jungle.

I turn to go back into the house. Jessica Ng is walking down the block, pushing a stroller. She's wearing black short shorts, a white halter top, and is absolutely, stunningly beautiful. In the six months I've lived here, she's the only neighbor I haven't spoken to. She scares me. She reminds me of a girl I loved in Saigon. I hurry off to my garage to watch her.

She crosses the street and stops at Tom's house. She calls to him in Vietnamese. Tom looks up from his gardening and calls back. He continues working and talking to her in Vietnamese. I'm astounded. I knew he had been in Nam, but I had no idea he could speak it. What little I knew, I knew from bar girls. How he knows what he knows, I have no idea—and I don't think I want to either. After a few minutes Tom walks towards her, carrying a bouquet of flowers. He gives her the flowers, then picks up her baby and holds him. The next several minutes I putter around my garage almost stunned: Tom spends more time on her kid than he does with Jessica. For all it matters to him she might as well not even be there. He carries the baby into his garden and leaves Jessica out on the street.

❖

Out back, Evan and Wendy are rolling around on the grass, banging into each other, then away. Willie's throwing the ball in the air and catching it. I decide to make a lumberjack breakfast for the two of us. In deference to Vicki I don't cook any bacon or sausage. I love the stuff, but she hates it whenever I let him eat junk food. "Nitrates-and-sugar-and-all-those-preservatives-and-dyes-make-him-all-hyper-active." "Good." I say, "Let him bust loose. Teach him to come in spikes high!" I look at the clock on the wall. It's getting late. Just about now, I figure, Vicki and her mom are sitting at one of those ferny places eating wheat germ or granola, some fiber-rich something or other that tastes like shredded wallboard, drinking decaffeinated dishwater coffee and talking about me as if I were the missing link between the Java Man and Stanley Kowalski.

I have two sweet rolls heating in the oven for just the hell of it. The pancake batter is ready and I'm debating about fruit, when I spot a broom in the corner next to the fridge. I walk over to it and turn it over. Sure enough, it's a screw-in handle. I unscrew it and stand there holding the stick. It's Brooklyn thirty-five years ago: hands sticky wet in the eighty percent humidity; Russ Hodges in the background calling the play-by-play as the Giants face the Dodgers at the Polo Grounds....Two on, one out, and the Giants are down by two. Dad's pitching. He's throwing as fast as he can. "No hitter," he keeps calling. "No hitter." I take a practice swing, another. I watch the spin of the Spalding as he throws a high, hard one right at my head and brushes me back from the plate. He's aiming for me, trying to scare me. I lean away and laugh, already knowing the outcome. I'm Bobby Thompson and he's Ralph Branca, and I'm going to take him deep. The next pitch is another fastball, and I step into it with all my might. I step into it, uppercutting it, shifting my weight. I use hip action and wrists, my own combination of Ted Williams and Charlie Lau, and swing a full 360 degrees and smash it...! crashing the top of the vase that Vicki's mom gave us for our ninth anniversary right through the frosted pink glass of the clock. My God! Jesus Christ! I stand there shaking. Then I start screaming along with Hodges, "The Giants win the pennant! The Giants win the pennant! The Giants win the pennant!" And I flip Ralph Branca the bird.

Evan races into the kitchen, yelling, "Mom! Mom!" and looks around. The broomstick is still in my hand. He shakes his head. "Mom's not going to be happy." I wince and shake mine. "But I won't tell," he adds. I smile and bend at the knees, just like my namesake, Stan-the-Man. I hold the stick steady, until I feel it start to move. It wiggles on its own, alive, a divining rod. I take a practice swing, another, grab my crotch, and point at the vase like the great Bambino pointing his finger at the bleachers. Evan covers his eyes and ducks under the table as I swing and twist myself into a corkscrew. The rest of the vase shatters all over the kitchen. "Yahoooo," I yell and drop the broomstick and run around the table doing my home-run trot. Evan watches me all big eyes. I wink at him and give him the thumbs up sign. He knows what this means, and he comes out from under the table and we slap each other a low five. "Yahooo," I yell again. Evan folds his arms across his chest and grins as I run around the table in circles.

Vicki wasn't pleased when Evan told her.

"Why did you make him lie?" she asks.

"I didn't *make* him. *He* said he wouldn't tell. Why'd you push him? A boy shouldn't snitch on his dad!"

"Snitch! What snitch—because he told his mother the truth. Come on, Stan, get real."

Six months ago I never heard those words "get real." Now I hear them every day. Six months ago I couldn't have told you the difference between tofu and toe jam, and now I can and I'm sorry.

I look out the window. The kids are running through Tom's sprinkler. Tom is sitting on his steps reading a magazine. He's wearing lime green running shorts and a pink and yellow tank top. He is the best-preserved, best-looking, most athletic guy on the block, and he's an absolute 100 percent fruitcake. He tosses the kids a Frisbee, stands, then bends, and stretches. Jesus, what must his father think! I know what my dad would do if I turned that way. He'd trounce me, then bounce me. No way he'd let me do that to him. Imagine! You have a son, you raise him, you do what you think is best, and he turns out to be like that. The thought of it gives my willies, the willies. I open the window and call:

"Evan, come on home."

He walks over to the window and looks up at me. "Yeah, Dad?" My heart stops. He's a lamb. Even when we play Monopoly he has no taste for the jugular. He'd rather loan you money than wipe you out. "Let's go out back and have a catch."

He looks over at Wendy and Willie playing Frisbee in the sprinkler. "I don't feel like it right now," he says.

I don't feel like it either, but it's something I think we should do. "It's either that or your room," I say.

In no time at all, we're tossing the ball back and forth and I'm telling him what to do. "High pop-up, use two hands." Evan circles around under it and drops it. "Slow roller. Charge it." He races in, scoops it up barehanded, and tosses the ball into the bushes. "Sorry," he says, "lost my grip." "Hard bouncer–don't be afraid.... No, no. You play the ball, don't let the ball play you...."

"I slipped...The sun...My shoes...It hit a rock." I can't stand all the phony excuses. I throw the ball faster and faster, moving him in and out, all over the yard. He's ragged, exhausted, sweating, breathing hard. "Couple more," I say, "and we'll quit." I throw a hard grounder over towards the tool shed. I want to see him backhand one. He moves for it, looks for the shed, and trips.

"Ok?" I call.

He doesn't move.

"Hey! Evan!" I walk over to him. His hands are covering his head and he's not moving. I panic–I've hurt him. I'm about to call Vicki when he moves his hands and gets up. His face is all wet and his eyes are red, his lower lip is quivering. "Evan," I say, putting my arm over his shoulders, "there's nothing to cry about. It's only for fun, for Christ's sake."

We're sitting in the kitchen cooling off. Vicki's drinking iced tea, I have a Pepsi, and Evan has a glass of fresh orange juice. I look at my watch. The game goes on in four hours. Evan gets up, finishes his juice, and washes his glass. "Can I go over to Tom's?" he asks. "He's watching Wendy and Willie for Helen." Vicki nods yes. "Of course," she says. I take my Pepsi into the den.

A month ago I told Vicki I wanted to go to these games. "It's going to be like '51 again," I told her. "It's going to go down to the wire."

"What's 51?" she said.

I told her all about Thompson and Branca and the stretch and the streak and the thirteen and a half games the Giants were out and how everyone in my family was a Dodger and I was a Giant and how my dad started screaming, "Shit! No! Shit! Don't bring in Branca!" and I started screaming "Branca! Branca! We want Branca!" and the whole house and block and neighborhood, the world, went nuts when Thompson hit the ball and Hodges started yelling, "The Giants win the pennant! The Giants win the pennant," and I started yelling it too, and my dad got so mad he snarled at me for what seemed like forever, and I snarled back and he punched me so hard I cried. Then I gave her the dates and said I was going to get tickets for her and Evan and me.

"But that's when I'm taking my vacation," she said. "I-want-to-go-to-the-mountains-or-Joshua-Tree-I-want-to-do-something-in-nature." What could I say? Chavez Ravine has real grass. The Giants are naturals. For my vacation we went to the Winter Olympics. So what could I do, I relented. Then two weeks ago she tells me her plans changed. She just has too much to do. "You-should-get-the-tickets-if-you-still-want-them." Still want them! Sure I still want them. Only they've been sold out now for weeks. I pick up the paper and re-read the standings, stats, and box scores. I want to make sure I haven't forgotten a thing.

"Dad! Dad!" Evan comes racing into the house, shouting.

"What is it?" I say, sitting up.

"Tom's friend came by and gave him two tickets to tonight's game. They were all supposed to go together but he can't and Tom asked me to ask you if we can go with him and Wendy and Willie." Vicki smiles. It's her "See-if-you-wait-what's-supposed-to-happen-will-happen" smile, and says, "I'll pack you fellows something to eat." I know better than to argue. We'll just dump the stuff at the park and get some hot dogs and soda and peanuts.

I go across the street and thank Tom and offer to drive, but he says, "No, I'd rather," and that's just fine with me. I'm too excited anyway. All the way there I keep saying, "It's going to be 1951 again," which none of them is too happy to hear: they're Dodgers and I'm still a Giant, and history's on my side.

Our seats are terrific, field level on the third-base side. I nudge Evan, who's talking to Wendy, who's sitting on his other side. "Good thing you brought your glove. This is a great spot to catch a ball."

Then I tell him about the time I caught one. I know I've told him this story, but I want him to hear it again. "A dozen people dove for it, including this really big guy who was sitting next to me and who actually had his hands on it. I got it away from him, though, in the tangle. My dad put it on the mantle with the family mementos. I think he still has it even now."

I look down the row at Wendy and Willie and Tom. "Anyone hungry?" I yell, "I'm buying! Whatever anyone wants!" I take all the orders and come back carrying everything. Evan, of course, wants nothing. The Rossini side packs it away as if there is no tomorrow, and Evan eats like Vicki—a squirrel. I bring him something anyway.

"Here," I say, "have a hot dog."

"Uh-uh," he says. "Mom won't like it."

"Then don't tell her."

He shrugs. I'd be happier if he said, "Fuck you." I look all around us. Everyone is eating hot dogs and popcorn and ice cream and Cracker Jack, drinking beer and soda and wine, and my son is peeling an egg. My God, what has Vicki done?

By the seventh inning the game is a blow-out. The Giants are ahead 8-3. The others are all dejected. Willie is talking to Tom and Evan is talking to Wendy. Nobody is watching the game—so I start talking to Evan about maybe catching a ball. A few have already come close. "You have to be ready," I tell him. "You have to pounce. As soon as you spot it, jump!" And just as I'm telling him this, one comes. "Go Evan! Get it! Dive! Grab it." And miracle of miracles, he emerges from the pile with the ball. I'm beaming. I'm proud. My kid's a hitter. "Stand up," I say, "and wave." The fans all around us cheer. It takes me a while to hear Wendy crying. "It's my ball," she says, "I had it first."

I put my arm around Evan and hug him. "Way to go, slugger," I say, and Wendy begins to wail. Tom and Willie try to calm her, but she only wails louder and louder. She continues for over an inning, with Evan looking back and forth from Wendy and Tom to me. "We'll put it on the mantle," I tell him, "We'll make it a Rossini family tradition," and I reach out to clutch him to me, and in that instant, that twitch, that blink of a nothing that separates the past and the future, he bares his teeth and growls at me with what I swear is rage without beginning or end.

On the way back to the car Evan keeps reaching for Tom's hand. Tom holds it, then drops it, then holds it, and drops it. I'm embarrassed that he's embarrassed for me. Evan bunches up his jacket and squeezes it close to his stomach. He's pretending he still has the ball—that it's rolled up safely inside—and when we get home he'll pretend that he lost it, that it fell out of his pocket or something. It could work—only I saw him give it to Wendy. What I don't know is what to do about it: Yell at him? Hug him? Ignore him? Forget it? Vicki would know—and so would my dad.

The ride back is eerily quiet. The kids fall asleep almost immediately, and Tom and I have nothing to say. We make a few attempts with the game and coming from the East, but neither of us has his heart in it. He turns the radio on to some classical station. I look out the window and read all the signs. Back home I thank him again for the tickets and for driving and offer to help him with Wendy and Willie. "That's ok," he says, and we shake and say, "Good night." I lift Evan out of the car and carry him upstairs and put him to bed. I'm exhausted but unable to sleep. I look in on Vicki—she's sleeping the sleep of the innocent. I go back to Evan. He's half out of bed and tangled in sheets. I pull him back and straighten him out, then go downstairs and walk all around the house looking out each of the windows. Every light in the neighborhood is out. It's pitch black.

Everyone is sleeping but me. I go back upstairs, undress, and slide into bed next to Vicki. I lift her arm and drape it over me, and I lie there, eyes open, looking at darkness, waiting for light. The last thing I remember before I fall asleep is how hard my father punched me.

Fantasy

Donna

Here's what she knows about Eric.

He doesn't look taken or attached. She's not sure how she knows this but she does. It could be the way he doesn't ogle women but looks at them directly, honestly, head-on, and the careful yet scruffy way he dresses—recent LA, not New York: jeans and rolled-up jacket sleeves; bright-colored shirts, mostly patterned, sometimes ethnic, always cotton or silk, and now and then a tie, but never a serious one, a dead trout, dollar signs, tiny Nixons. His shoes are Mephistos, never scuffed and never shined, just worn natural like him. His hair is California too, loose and shaggy, Hollywood-manicured to look unruly, a little too long in the front. He wears French glasses for reading. LaCoste. Green frames that offset his blue eyes and black almost Asian hair, though he's definitely not Asian—Greek or Hungarian maybe, or Basque, something exotic she's sure. His chin reminds her of Michael Douglas's and he's got a marvelous tan.

He always carries a briefcase with him, not the square-edged kind that's combination-locked and hard-leathered, but a soft, custom-made satchel with his name, ERIC, engraved on the straps. In it he has a laptop, cellular phone, loose papers, and two or three books. She's seen him use the phone once to make a quick call when their train was delayed at Jamaica. He's never taken the laptop out, but she saw it when he opened his bag. He's always reading something, not a newspaper or magazine but a book by someone she's never heard of. She has no idea what he does.

People like him, though, she can tell. He smiles easily and often, and he laughs and talks to everyone around him. Once the seat next to him was vacant. She almost took it, but she'd spent the evening at Carl's and was tired and didn't look or smell her best. Ever since then she's been dressing for him every Monday, Wednesday, and Friday, hoping she'd get her chance.

ERIC

He makes it to the 7:25 at Bayshore just in time. He's been commuting every Monday, Wednesday, and Friday morning for the past three months and is starting to hate it. During the summer it was wonderful, but it's early October now, and the days are shorter, and he resents the extra hour and a half it takes him to get to the office than it would if he left from his place. This morning, though, he's enthused about going to work.

He's going to tell Marsha his story: that he lives in Bayshore, on the Bay, and that he has a place on Fire Island and another in Manhattan in the Sixties on the upper East Side and that he wants her to see all of them, starting with this weekend at Fire Island. It's a story he doesn't tell often but one that he likes to tell. It's his job to know what a good story is—and this one, he knows, is good. Much better than saying he is housesitting for one of his clients and that the house on Fire Island is part of the deal and that the place in Manhattan where he regularly lives is a one-room studio walk-up he shares with a lawyer friend who uses it occasionally as a weekend *pied-à-terre* with his mistress and pays half of the twelve hundred dollar-a-month rent for the right. If he and Marsha wind up going out long enough—which, in this case, is December 15, when his client returns—and she learns the truth, then at that point it shouldn't matter. And if they don't, well, who cares?

He removes a book from his bag and leaves the bag on the seat next to the window. He takes off his jacket, folds it over the bag, stretches his legs out in front of him, and begins to read. He's trying to keep the seat next to him vacant—at least until Freeport, where the puff-lipped redhead gets on the train. They've been looking at each other for a week now, and the last time he smiled at her, she smiled back. No big deal, just flirting, but nice.

He spreads his legs to hold onto the space. Freeport is four stops away. At Wantagh, people begin eyeing the seat, but he keeps his head down and legs spread, and no one is willing to ask. At Bellmore, a woman does. "Excuse me," she says. He shuts his book, places his jacket on his lap and lowers his bag to the floor—without looking up. He's about to stand to let her pass, when he changes his mind and slides over and takes the window seat for himself. It'll be easier for her and better for him: the light is much brighter for reading. He opens his book, resumes reading—and immediately feels her staring.

He looks at her in the glass. She isn't bad-looking at all. He didn't see her when she first sat down, but now he sees that she's very well dressed and made up. Out of the corner of his eye he sees her hands folded on her lap and her crossed calves. Her nails are long, sculpted, and pointed, which tells him she's probably not a secretary. They're all painted plum except for the left pinky, which is glossy black and glittery. Her jewelry is simple and tasteful—silver rings and bracelet, pearl necklace, and a diamond stud in her ear. He likes that, though he senses she's too ordinary and uninventive for him. She's probably in some kind of sales, which is why she dresses so well: it's required, and she buys on discount. She has a great pair of legs, though, and fabulous silver-blonde hair. He moves his bag and jacket to give her more room.

"Thanks," she says. "What are you reading? The cover is very distinctive."

"I chose it."

He goes on to tell her he's a lawyer and a literary agent. The books he reads are by people he represents. This one is by a Russian no one has ever heard of but who really knows how to write.

At Freeport he watches for the puff-lipped redhead and doesn't see her get on the train–at least not on his car–not that it matters. He's enjoying himself flirting with this one. She's so obviously interested in him. He takes it as a sign, an omen, like making the 7:25, sitting in this seat and meeting her–Donna–that the rest of his day is going to be perfect. At Penn Station he walks with her up the stairs. She's going uptown, he's going across. "See you on Monday," she says, then smiles and bites at her lip.

He doubts it–but you never know. He tucks her away as "A Possible," in case everything else falls through.

MARSHA

It's 7:50 and she's going to be late. She's standing in the shower and considering phoning work and taking off. Nick wants her to–and she wants to, too. They woke up and made love like they used to–early in the morning–and after last night and their fight and Nick's coming home late, she thinks she really should. It would be good for her–for THEM. It would. Only she hasn't had this job even a month–and there's a thousand people who would take it on a snap–and she also has that lunch she agreed to a week ago when she and Nick were fighting. Now she wishes it wasn't today. She feels a little hypocritical: last night she accused Nick of cavorting, and today she's going out to lunch.

She feels funny about it anyway. He's not her boss exactly—but he is over her. What if she'd said no? What would have happened? And now, now that she's said yes, what's next? He is attractive and articulate and funny but isn't her type. She's seen him with clients: with the famous ones he's a little too soft and fawning, and with the newer up-and-comers like Sergei, he takes advantage when he doesn't need to and exaggerates to win his points.

Nick comes into the bathroom, lifts the seat, and begins to pee. She likes to watch him standing naked, his legs spread and shaking it off. He finishes and reaches for the handle.

"Don't," she calls.

He turns the light off and pulls the curtain back, steps into the tub, kneels and licks her. His tongue and the water on her body feel perfect. He turns her around and he soaps her, making her his all over again. He wants her to stay home. That's what he's asking.

She thinks about it while she's drying herself. She thinks about it while brushing her teeth, blow-drying her hair, and putting on make-up. She thinks about it while choosing what she's going to wear, and while dressing, and on the way to work while Nick drives her—all the way, a first—to the building door, where he double-parks, walks with her, hugs her, kisses her, and wishes her a good day. She thinks about it in the elevator—from the lobby to the 85th floor—and down the marbled hallways, through the oak doors, all the way to her desk in the back. All morning she thinks about it, going home sick and spending the day making love with Nick. She thinks about it right up until noon, when her phone rings and she hopes, really hopes, that it's him and that he'll actually come right out and ask so that then she could do what she wants.

"How about the Quilted Giraffe?"

"Sure. Whatever. I'm ready."

"Right there. I'm revisiting Sergei's contract."

She's relieved. At least there's no chance of running into Nick, but if she does, she'll just tell him the truth: she had to have lunch with her boss. It isn't her fault, is it, that he's thirty-fivish, talented, single, handsome, and tanned? During lunch she'll probe him with questions, though she knows she won't have to work very hard. She wants to hear his story, all of it, especially the details. She already knows he's a young man on the move, the son of a Las Vegas car dealer, trying to make it big in the Apple—but specifics will make him more real, so that when she tells Nick all about him he'll believe her and get really jealous. Maybe then he'll appreciate her for who she is, the way Eric does.

Nick

He gave it his best, he did. Love in the morning, breakfast, shower together, even a ride downtown. She knew what he was saying, she did. She knew it and paid him no mind. Now he's on his way to see Gloria. Not yet, though. Her busiest time is before noon, and they were out late together last night. Recently, he's become infatuated with her. He met her when he bought Marsha her birthday gift. He spent over an hour joking with Gloria about lingerie and other sexy and silly things. He liked her sense of humor and the ease with which he could talk with her, the way she understood what he meant—and now how she thinks he's really funny, smart, talented, and frank. She's from Cuba. She's dark. Intriguing. Fiery, he imagines. A lover of heat. One of the reasons he and Marsha have stopped making love in the morning is that after she leaves for work, he dreams about Gloria and masturbates: her arms around him, her legs; her tongue on every piece of his skin. *Every* piece. Until last night, though, it was fantasy. Gloria's boyfriend, Franco, is an Italian who has family on

Mott Street, and that could mean trouble for Nick. He's seen enough Mafia movies to know that much. Yesterday, though, Gloria told him that she and Franco were over. They spent most of last night drinking Cuervo and Coke at Victor's, talking about Franco and Marsha as if they were dead.

This morning he wants to see her a lot, but he's never, ever, seen her two days in a row. Yesterday, he feels, was a breakthrough. It was the first time he was able to be honest with himself about Marsha. She's just too demanding and insecure—a dreadful combination. He knows the reasons, knows all about her childhood, her parents' accident, and her being raised by a doting and lavishing godmother who gave her everything for nothing. But knowing the reasons is not enough. He has to be with who she is right now, and right now he'd rather be with Gloria. Of course, he has been here before, which is how he first started seeing Marsha when he and Louise were breaking up. And before Louise there was Allyson. Anyhow, Gloria will be different, because—well, she's different. He can hardly wait till he sees her.

Gloria

She wants to be a Hollywood actress. Until then, she's in sales—where she meets all kinds of interesting people. She's amazed at what people tell her, especially the men. They'll reveal anything personal, the more personal the better, just to get her attention, which is why she doesn't trust any of them. But she feels ok with Nick. He's like a brother. She can talk to him, and he doesn't try or think any funny stuff. Like last night, just talking about her and him and Franco and Marsha, and he didn't make any moves. Men always do that with her. It's hard for her to say no. It's as if she's a guest and it would be rude or impolite. She never wants to believe that it's happening—even though it does nearly all the time—but by the time she sees it coming, it's always too late. Not that she *has* to do anything, not that they'd hurt her if she didn't, it's just that she feels obliged. Especially if they've been nice to her or bought her something or treated her very well—the way Franco did when she first arrived from Cuba. Franco says she should change her clothes and makeup and then men wouldn't come on to her, but when she's with him that's all he wants her to be. He likes her to be the center—the sexiest woman around—and he buys her the sexiest things. Then afterwards he yells at her and treats her like dirt.

She wishes Franco was nice to her like Nick, or that Nick looked as good to her as Franco—or that Sal told her *before* she liked him that he was married to Rose. But that's how it is for her, half-and-half, never the whole. Meanwhile, there's this black lacey halter that just came into the store, and if it looks on her like she thinks it will, she's going to get it and wear it dancing at the Fugazi tonight and drive Sal and Franco nuts.

FRANCO

He loves his Gloria. He really does. He wants to cherish her, protect her, care for her—do everything. Keep her home—except for parties and dancing where she likes to be the shiniest lady in sight. His parents, though, won't tolerate her. His mother even called her a *puta*. It's because she's not Italian and the way she dresses. They want him to marry Anna, a third-generation Italian-American, who was once Miss Little Italy and whose father has political ties and is a power broker with the Republican Party.

Franco doesn't know what to do, although he knows he'll do what his parents want. What else can he do? He'll do like his father: have his Gloria on the side and marry Anna–who is pining for Brent, who's sorry he left Carol, who's still missing David, who's masturbating over Edie, who's trying to leave Frank, who secretly loves Gem, who's been promised to Hu, who dreams about Isabel, who lives with Jon, who's sending anonymous love letters to Karen, who's experimenting with Lynne, who really likes Michaela, who used to be Mike, and then there is Nan, who has given up completely, bought a pug and a Manx, and is unreservedly, unhappily celibate.

I Saw a Man Hit His Wife

It was last month. I'm sure it was his wife because I overheard parts of their conversation, and it was normal, ordinary husband-wife kind of talk about children, work, friends, what video to watch after dinner—the kinds of things people who have been together a long time talk about without listening or thinking. There wasn't any rancor, tension, or edge. Several times I looked over at them because they were laughing so hard I wanted to know what was funny. You never really know what's underneath, do you? Nothing is solid anymore. You expect one thing and something else starts seeping out.

I wasn't paying them *that* much attention. I was there at Francine's with Sunny to celebrate our twelfth anniversary, and we were discussing the same sorts of things as they were. I overheard parts of their conversation when there was a lull in our own. Francine's is French, listed and well known, with three or four stars, depending on the reviewer and the publication. It's the place you go in this town if you have something to celebrate and you don't want to go to the city. Everything was proper as usual, the restaurant, the other customers, me in my Ivy look, navy blazer and gray slacks, and Sunny in her cobalt-blue silk and onyx. We looked good, but the couple next to us looked wonderful. He looked like Robert Redford, only darker. He wore a European-cut double-breasted charcoal-and-silver pinstripe with a black silk shirt buttoned at the neck. It was very, very distinctive—how I'd like to look, but can't. I'm too slight and fair. He must have been fifty or fifty-five and was totally self-possessed. She was a little younger, forty-five maybe, and was built and moved like a model, long and thin and graceful—one of those people who are very comfortable being watched. She wore a long purple skirt, wide leather belt, hand-tooled, and more silver and turquoise on her fingers, up her wrists, around her neck, and through her ears than I've ever seen in my life. I saw them when they first drove up in a brand-new maroon Jaguar XS. I watched him park and open the door for her and lead her into the restaurant. I watched as Michael sat them at the corner table nearest to us. They began with a hundred-dollar bottle of Mumm's. I don't know what they were celebrating, but it certainly seemed to be something—and it certainly seemed very nice.

Francine's used to be a Catholic church—I've eaten there so often that I almost forgot. It used to be St. John the Divine. Francine bought it from the diocese and turned it into a restaurant, naming it after herself. She kept the stations-of-the-cross frescos, the upstairs choir loft where the bar is, and what was left of the stained glass windows. Over the years she's changed the food from classic French to nouvelle cuisine to country, and this year the dishes and silverware are new. Sunny doesn't like the changes. If it was up to her, she'd keep the place exactly the same. She's not that way about everything. She's usually the one who initiates change. But on certain occasions she prefers ritual: same place, same wine, same table—which is why we were there. I would have gone to the city.

It was while we were having dessert, sharing a *crème brûlée,* that I heard him call her a cunt. He said it so softly, so kindly, caressingly almost, that it sounded like a term of endearment. I looked up and saw him smile, then saw the flash of his ring. His hand was midway across the table holding a cigarette. He put the cigarette down and smiled, then held his hand in the air as if to make a gesture and reached over and smacked her mouth. His ring must have caught her upper lip because I saw a little line of blood appear, first slowly, almost imperceptible against the dark, deep red of her lipstick, but then it bubbled and slid over her teeth and into her mouth. She sat there calmly as if she'd just been confirmed, looking at him and nodding, her cheek dappling like roseate marble. He reached over and patted her lip with his napkin, he dipped the tip of his napkin into his water glass then pressed it against her lip to stop the bleeding and gently wiped the blood away. It all happened so quickly it was like watching a stolen kiss.

I don't think anyone else but Sunny and me saw it. Sunny just shrugged and said, "Love." In matters of devotion she's much more tolerant than I am. What I wanted to know was who was right and who was wrong and what is it that deserves a slap? Maybe it was too mild. Maybe it was severe. How do you know? Who's to say? These things are not easy to judge. Sunny lifted my hand from my wine glass, brought it to her mouth and held it there kissing my palm. I pulled it away, embarrassed. It used to be you could never, ever, under any circumstances, hit a woman. But now it's only the circumstances that count.

Here's something else I've been thinking about lately. When I was a boy and the picture on the television began to flutter sideways or up and down, my dad would get up and switch through the channels, turning the knob backwards and forwards very fast. If that didn't stop the picture from moving, he'd bang the set on its side. Sometimes he'd use the flat of his hand, sometimes a rolled-up newspaper. Sometimes he'd hit one side, sometimes the other, and sometimes, though not very often, the top.

"How do you know," I'd ask him, "what to do? When to hit it, where, and how hard?"

His answer was always the same. "You do whatever works."

To a whole other set of questions, my mother would say,

"Whatever makes you happy, so long as no one gets hurt."

Oh yes, it once was as simple as that. And now? Now nothing is simple or easy or clear. My wife Sunny likes me to hit her. Not like the guy in the restaurant—she wouldn't like that and I wouldn't do it if she did. There are limits. You just have to know them for yourself and find them. Sunny likes me to hit her in bed. We've been doing it once maybe twice a month now for years. Still, there's a part of me that resists. Which part, I often wonder, my better self, my more humane, the Spinoza that's left in me, or the chicken, as Sunny calls it, the part that's afraid to cross over and see the other side?

The first time it happened was a fluke—at least I think it was. It was during the Iran-Contra hearings when every day for months a different White House spokesperson explained how they hadn't actually done what they did. It was at the time when everywhere you looked, all the magazines, fashion designers, ads, tv shows, models, rock and Hollywood stars, everything and everyone was flirting with S & M and B & D. Leather, studs, spikes, chains, whips, handcuffs, razors, safety pins, leashes, collars, medieval attire, you name it. It was while we were in bed watching Donahue, taped from that afternoon—his guests were three S & M couples dressed in leather and studs and tattoos—that Sunny kissed my ear, then bit it and whispered, "Spank me."

"Why?" I said.

Sunny shook her head and shrugged. "I just want you to."

I wavered at the time, I still do, but I did it, I spanked her and have done worse things since. That's the thing about boundaries. Once you cross them they no longer exist. I don't know why that is, it just is. Every time you push past one, you wonder what's further, what's next—how far you can go before you fall off this Earth?

❖

The other day at work I made a list of things I'd never do. I'd never hit Sunny in the face, never really hurt her, leave any visible marks or bruises, humiliate her, or do anything in public. What Sunny won't do, I can't fathom. She hates going to the dentist or getting shots. She won't see psychological horror films or those made for tv abuse stories. She doesn't like pornography, and if she wasn't such a liberal, she'd just as soon have it all banned. A week ago she came home crying and angry because it was reported that the mother of her best student was being severely beaten on a regular basis by her ex. Then later that night she cooed me into slapping her breasts and her thighs with a brand-new mahogony brush that she'd bought that afternoon for the occasion. "I am full of contradictions," she said to me afterwards. "I am large." She was quoting Whitman–she often does. I would have chosen Poe.

Officially, Sunny and I aren't married. I call her my wife and she calls me her husband because that's how we live and feel. We've been together now almost thirteen years. We're married in every way but the church and the law: she's on my health plan, I'm on hers; the house and cars are jointly owned. Timothy, her son, is like my own. We say we are married because we like to, and because in this town, if we weren't and lived like this, neither one of us could hold our jobs. Sunny's a medievalist, teaching modern world history at the high school. My degrees are in English and philosophy. I work as a supervisor for Goodwill. We've lived here now for eight years. We left the city and all of its troubles behind. We couldn't take it anymore, the selfishness, brutality, the lies; Mayor Goode obliterating a neighborhood in order to save it. For what? Whom? When?

Sunny's given name is Katie O'Connell. She's Irish-Catholic, ex-Catholic, lapsed. I was brought up Unitarian. Sunny calls it Utilitarian. "Humiliation," I tell her, "comes natural to you."

The last time I said it she looked at me and shook her head. "You really *don't* get it, do you? You don't have the power. *I'm* giving myself to you."

Of course I don't get it. To me it's the Inquisition—tie 'em up and beat 'em until they relent. "I've *already* relented," she laughs. "This isn't about control, it's abandonment. Total abandon. I'm giving up completely. It's bliss."

I try to make light of it, but I can't. What am I doing, hitting a woman—the person I love more than anyone else in this world? I couldn't even punish Timothy when he went through my things and "borrowed" the ID bracelet my father gave me and lost it. I haven't been in a single fight since I was a boy. I've never hit anyone until Sunny. I joke and tell her it's because she's one-quarter German and she feels guilty about the war. I tell her it has to do with those prurient priests, brittle nuns, and purple holy cards, with being a medievalist. I've told her it's a sign of the times, your basic end-of-a-millennium activity: scarring, branding, crystals, body piercings, psychic hotlines, beatings, and other prerational and antediluvian ways people have of trying to locate themselves. But nothing I say matters—her answer's the same: "I'm so excited. I've never been so happy in all of my life."

The closest she's come to explaining it to me is with the Pentacosts and their flagellations. "It's not punishment they sought, it was rapture. Why do you think it was condemned? It was an ecstasy of the flesh as well as the spirit. They did it because they loved Jesus completely, with their *bodies* and souls."

"And you, what do you do it for?"

"Me. Me and you—just us."

I don't know if I understand this or not. There's *nothing* I'd give myself up to that way except maybe doubt. I'm not even sure what I'd do if someone came into the house with a gun or a knife and raped her. Would I intercede? Would I be willing to stand up and die or get beaten or crippled to stop it? I don't know. I really don't know. I love her, but in a way so different from her love for me.

I've thought about her childhood. I've thought about her life. Is there hidden guilt? Anger? Self-loathing? Shame? I've looked and searched for cracks.

"Have you ever done this with anyone else?"

"No," she smiles. "No one else has ever deserved me this way."

What can you say to that? I don't know. She overwhelms me. I've started to read books about it. Sunny laughs when she sees me. "That's the philosopher's way. Study it to death. Make it an intellectual issue."

"I just want to understand."

"There's *nothing* to understand. I've told you. It's desire—the blind passion of Saint Joan, Henry Miller in Paris, Van Gogh. It's faith. Understanding will tell you nothing. It's not epistemology or psychology. It's theology without a church, and I am God."

She may be right, but my world is different from hers. Hers allows you anything as long as you continue to believe. Mine forgives you nothing; it's a world of cause and effect and of consequences: $E = mc^2$.

Sunny says I should give myself up and cross over. She says she'll do whatever she can to help. But I don't think I want to. Every day in the papers and on tv I see abuse, rape, wife beating, the terrible way men treat women in our world. Sunny says what we do is not the same. Sunny says *my* pleasure comes from my doubt, which is why, she says, I worry it to death. She's right, and she's wrong. My pleasure also comes from giving her pleasure. All I want in this life is to please her. I'd never do anything to harm her, I couldn't live with myself if I did. The truth is, I love her so much that I bend.

Today is my forty-fifth birthday. Sunny will have something excessive planned–she always does. Last year she gave me an antique black silk kimono and a pair of sterling-silver handcuffs; the year before a two-foot-long braided gold key chain that doubled as a leash for the choke collar she bought for herself. She's in the bathroom now getting ready. Timothy's at his dad's for the night, and we've already been to Francine's, where Sunny kept recalling the last time we were there when the man hit his wife. I'm sitting on the edge of the bed, in candlelight, just waiting, surrounded by the implements I'll later use: belts of different widths and materials, leather, lacing, her brush, a vibrator, dildos, wooden clothespins, nipple clamps, and the handcuffs she gave me last year.

The door opens and I'm submerged in light. Sunny's wearing the white silk Chinese pajamas and the magenta kimono I gave her twelve years ago for our first anniversary. She stands in the doorway, backlit, with her hands behind her, looking radiant, alive in a way she only looks on evenings like this. She's strong, brazen, jubilant. There's not a doubt about her. She's as secure as I am lost.

"For you," she says, stepping forward and handing me a black-and-white-wrapped package from behind her back.

It's so light and thin it surprises me. It's about twelve inches long and five inches wide. I shake it, hear nothing, and see the pattern on the wrapping paper change shape as the box moves through the light. I shake it again and start to open it.

"No," she says. "Not yet."

She turns the bathroom light off and walks to the bed. She picks up the handcuffs and gives them to me, then puts her hands behind her back and turns around. I place the cuffs snugly on her wrists and clasp them. As each one locks she goes, "Mmmmmmmm." She turns around and faces me. I'm slightly taller, but in the flickering candle-light and at the angle we're standing, I can barely see myself in the mirror behind her. "I love you," she says, and kneels and lowers her head. Then she looks up and smiles. "Now," she says. "Open it now."

The paper comes easily undone. I'm going slowly. I haven't figured out what's inside yet and I'm a little anxious. I lift the cover off the box and pull the tissue paper back and am relieved to see a pair of black leather gloves. I hold them up, then pull them on, first on my left hand, then my right. They're soft. Smooth. Tight. Thin. They're driving gloves. I smell them. "They're beautiful–a perfect fit." I hold my hands up in front of my face to show her and clap my palms together.

"Doeskin," she says. "Handstitched. From Morocco." She nods at me.

I bend over, run my fingers down her cheek, under her chin, and kiss her. "Mmmmmmm," she murmurs, "feels goood," and she tilts her head back and smiles at me, triumphant. I take her chin in my hand, hold it, and kiss her again. "Please," she says. "Honey, please." I touch her hair, kiss her ear, her neck, start to go for her mouth again but she turns away. I stop and look at her, holding my hands together in front of me as if I'm praying. She nods at me again, only harder, more like a yank, snapping her head back the way a horse does when it's tethered. "Please," she says, "Honey, please...." She sounds like she's going to cry. "Please." She's pleading, and suddenly I know what she wants. I lower my hands and squeeze them together tightly. I lock my fingers, cross my thumbs. A new line will be crossed if I do this, another boundary, and then this too will be added to our repetoire, and something irretrievable will have occurred; and I know this too: from this moment on, my life will be simpler and sadder. Compared to whose, I ask myself, unlinking my fingers and hoping I won't leave any marks, compared with what, now that nothing is fixed and I am free.

Jersey

You want I should tell you about Abie. Sixty years I know him.... A long time... The things I could tell you. You know the *Freiheit?* No? Of course not. By you it means nothing. Today, I should tell you, what we stood for means nothing to nobody. But this you don't want to hear. So, I promise, like they say in the movies, that I will stick to the facts.

One week ago we were sitting in his room playing chess just like we always did on Fridays. Abie loved to play. In the good weather we'd play outside–in the park or on the sidewalk. In the winter we'd play in his room. Abie wanted it like that. He used to say it was the only time since his Rosie passed that he enjoyed his room.... So, we were playing chess. That's the fact. Only Abie, he wasn't playing too good. Already in six moves he loses a pawn and a knight. To tell you the truth, I hadn't noticed before, but Abie, he didn't care about the game, and for him, I should tell you, that was something. So, Abela, I say, maybe you don't want to play. Maybe you want I should leave. Such a look he gives me. Such a look! Only when his Rosie passed had I seen it. Then I remembered in one week would be the anniversary of her death. So maybe, I'm thinking, Abie needs some cheering. That's when I ask him about Rosie. You see, we had this routine. You know what is a routine? Like Abbott and Costello. You know about them? Yes. Good. Well, we had a routine about Rosie. It went like this:

Abie, tell me again about Rosie.

She was beautiful, Herbie, beautiful. Remember?

I remember.

She was strong. Lungs she had like bellows. And arms! Not like these skinny things today. They're like sparrows. No, my Rosie was different. One tough buzzard. Never took from nobody.

Except you.

From me she had to. But even then, I should tell you, never much.

That Rosie.

She should rest in peace.

Zei gezunt.

She used to call me her Jewish Valentino, remember?

Sure I remember. You were her Jewish Valentino.

And you, you were her Eric Flynt.

That was our routine. Always in the past, it made Abie happy. That day, I could tell, it did nothing. In three more moves he loses the other horse. Abie, I say, something's wrong? That's when he tells me. Herbie, he says, I'm too old. Only me, I don't hear too good. I think he says he's cold. So, *nu?* I say. Don't be so cheap with the heat. Abie grins. I don't know why, but I do too. I like to see him smile. When he lost his teeth he stopped. Only with me he continues. For this you bought a hearing aid, he says. Switch it up. I want you to hear what I'm talking. I shut it off, you know, when we play chess. I don't want I should be distracted. And Abie, he knows this. He whistles before a good move. So I shut it off so as not to have to hear. But when he speaks, what I hear I am not expected for. I'm too old, he says. Not cold. Already I'm eighty-two years. My father, he should rest in peace, lived for sixty. My Rosie for seventy-three. I've seen enough. I don't want to see no more. *Farshstaist?* I don't want to see no more. Already after a few words I'm thinking, why is he telling me this? Why is he saying it? My Abela I know. From nothing he doesn't speak. So what by me does he want? Herbie, he says, you hear what

I'm talking? I hear, I tell him, but I don't believe. From such a mouth I never expected these words. For sixty years I know him. A *macher* he could have been. A big shot. And such a brain! I should tell you. From his mouth came only iron and pearls.... At Patterson, Gastonia, Brooklyn. You know what I'm talking? No? Such a shame. Always with him came a *L'chayam*. You know what is that? To life. Always when he spoke came *L'chayam*. At Patterson, Gastonia, Brooklyn.

So, Abela, I say, something's the matter? You're ill? Maybe you want we should talk? No, he says, nothing. Life is wonderful. In the morning I take a little walk and in a few short feet I'm exhausted. I read a little in the afternoon and my eyes they water and ache. Out of a can comes my supper. At night I go to sleep like a child at eight o'clock. And the next day I wake up for what? For what do I live? Pills that I take for the heart? A piece of beef I can't even enjoy with these *fishtinkiner* teeth? And what I see on television, nobody needs to see. So you see, Herbela, my life is fine. It's wonderful. Nothing is the matter. *L'chayam*, I say. No more, he says. This is not life. This is no way to live. The things in life that are important are not for me. So, I say, Mr. Revolutionary, oppression is all of a sudden over? To this I know he will react. The world is such a good place to live it no longer needs Abraham Isaac Hersch? This is so? You should tell me. Maybe I am missing. With news like this I'd willingly join you in the grave. Abie says nothing. *Nu?*

I say, *Nu?* The fight is over? Herbie, he says, I'm tired of staying the soldier. I don't even write any more my letters. So write! I say. Don't want, he says. No more. Instead of Abie getting angry, I am. So you're old. So am I. You think my life is better than yours? This, between us, is an old struggle. Always we compared our miseries. You, he says, at least have Esther. So, for years you had Rosie and I had *bopkes*. Now is the other way. Such is life. I don't want it, he says. So what do you want? You want I should call Sadie Pickens? Abie laughs. Better I should die a celibate. *Nu?* So what? What I want, he says, is for you to take me to Jersey.

As soon as he says this I smile. Always on personal items he talks around the bush, then bang! Apples he talks when he wants oranges, his Rosie used to say, but when he finishes I should tell you aleph to sof's been said. Used to be he called it the real *megillah*. You know what is that? The big picture. Rosie, she called it *shmaltz*. So Abela, I say, for years you don't leave Brooklyn—not since the march on the Pentagon. All the time I say, come to a museum, to a matinee show in the city? Come, a sandwich we'll get, a nice cup tea? No, you say, don't want. Don't want to go, don't want to see, not hungry, and now, from the blue, you want I should take you to Jersey? Abie knows I'm joking. But already he knows what I'm thinking. Always he knows what I'm thinking. By us, you see, Jersey means two things: Patterson and Mary O'Sheen, and Patterson I know he don't want. *Nu*? Abela? I say. You know where now is Mary? I know, he says, I know. And she wants to see you? She wants, she wants. Then he gives me that look. A week ago yesterday I called. To tell you the truth, when he says this I'm not surprised. On tactics and women Abie always did better than me.

So four days later I take him. I still drive, you know. A Buick. UAW-made. Abie is dressed like a king. He's wearing his blue serge, and his Florsheims I should tell you are so shiny you could see your face. Even he's got on a tie. And in his pocket, I see, is stuffed his Spanish beret. Used to be he called this his courtroom outfit. You know what I'm talking? Yes. Good. Last time he wore it he got ten days. If you was younger, the judge said, you'd get more. If I was younger, Abie said, I'd of done more. Then he gives to the judge such a speech on human rights the courtroom with a bang! applauded. But this you don't want to hear. To you this is nothing, *bopkes*. So now I return to the story. All the way there Abie is talking about Mary. Mary this. Mary that. Mary, *kineahora*, is still organizing. Nurses, orderlies, maids, people who work where she lives. That

Mary! Fifty years he knows her. Knows, not sees. This I assure you is a fact. Used to be he called her his Wild Irish Rose, till his Rosie made him stop. Then he called her Irish Emma. You know who is that, Emma Goldman? No? A little history you should read. It wouldn't hurt. Some Marx, some Lenin, a little Kropotkin. Believe me, I know what I'm talking. So, Abela, I say, when we arrive, you want that I should come? Better, he says, go get a nice cup tea.

Three hours later I come back. Abie is waiting on the curb. He knows I don't want to drive in the dark. So Abie, I say, how's Mary? Abie shrugs. She's good? Abie nods. You had, *kineahora,* a nice visit? Abie looks at me and says nothing, and for Abie, I should tell you that's something. Always about everything Abie has something to say. A regular encyclopedia he was. Abie, I say, is this you? On his face I see he remembers. Who else, he says, John D.? This, by us, was an old joke. Then he looks at me and says, We were right, Herbie, right about everything in our analysis, only we couldn't live what we believed.

You know what this means? I'll tell you. About this I know something about. Used to be Abie and Mary were lovers. In those days we believed in that. Smash the family, we said. Kill monogamy. Nobody should belong to nobody. Marriage and family are the backbone of the bourgeois state. So all of us then had many lovers. On principle. Rosie too. Only when she found her Abie with Mary and heard him call her his Wild Irish Rose, she stopped. No more, Abie, she told him. No more. I can't do. It's me or Mary O'Sheen. So from that day on, Abie never saw Mary again. But always I know he felt bad. Always I know he wanted to, but Rosie, she wouldn't let. So when Abie said we never could live what we believed, this is what he meant, and when he said he wanted to go to Jersey, I knew why he wanted to go. After this Abie says nothing. On the ride home he sits quiet like a clam, holding in his hands his beret.

The next Friday, like always, I'm going to his room to play chess.

Only Abie calls me and says don't come. This, I should tell you, is a first. I'm too busy, he says, come next week, we'll play. Too busy? I say. What's to be too busy about? The revolution is here and I'm missing? But Abie don't hear. Already he's hung up the phone. Then that night he gives me a call. Herbela, he says, come over, I'm sick. My Abie I know. About illness he don't complain. So quick as a whistle I come. Abie is already in bed. On his face I can see he is dying. Now, about this we had many talks. No doctors. No ambulance. No hospital. Whatever money, we leave to the poor. Abela, I say, you want something? Sure, he says, thirty years. Then he points with his hand to his desk. I want you should mail those letters. Three days, I see, he's been writing again, to the President, Congress, the Pentagon, Arafat, Mandela, Castro. My Abela, he's telling them what they should do. You'll mail? he says. I'll mail. There's no stamps, he says. I'll buy. Good, he says, this way I get the last word. Then he looks at me and whispers, *L'chayam.*

All night I sit with him. I don't want he should be alone. In the morning I go and buy some stamps. Thirty-five letters, can you believe? Then I mailed them and came back here and called you.

FATHER'S DAY

It astonishes me, the relationship between kids and their parents. You take a guy, an average guy, someone with nothing outstanding going for him—he may not even be nice. And there by his side is his kid. As far as the kid is concerned, this guy is the universe. All this kid wants is this guy's eye, his hand, a look, a hint, a whisper of some recognition. The guy touches the kid, rubs his head, takes his hand, and the kid looks at him as if he's in heaven....

I'm standing here in Grand Central Station seeing this. All around me the place is a zoo. Crazy people, wackos, weirdos, loonies, junkies, refugees from every sore and wound in the world, screeching at each other, babbling in words, sounds, grunts, gestures, pushing, humping, bumping, shoving for this reason or that or no reason. It's monstrous. Terrible. Frightening. It's an inferno—and this kid, this babe, this lamb, this innocent, feels safe because this guy is standing there right next to him. Nobody else in the world—not the guy's mother, not his wife, nobody—would find comfort in his being there. Some people move further away. He just *feels* vulnerable. If anybody's going to get hit this afternoon, he knows it's going to be him. But this kid—this seven-year-old boy—feels protected from God, the world, insanity, nature, from anything and everything as it all takes place in front of him beneath the grand stairway leading down from the stars. The kid looks up and sees none of it. He holds his father's hand and looks at him as if he's a hero with holy, unqualified love. It amazes me. I'm awestruck at the power, the authority, the grace children believe their parents have. It must be the reason people have kids.

I'm thinking about this because it's Father's Day. I've been thinking about my dad a lot. He was a big man, over six feet tall, and he had large hands and long fingers that were thick and strong. I remember how he used to toss me high in the air and catch me and put me on his shoulders and run. Mom would always run around after us, laughing, saying, "Careful, Joe, be careful." Careful when we wrestled. Careful when we played ball. "Careful, careful, don't be so hard and rough." But of course he never was hard and rough, and he never hurt me either.

I remember once looking into their bedroom and seeing my dad in his underwear standing in front of the mirror, flexing and strutting around for my mom. Mom saw me and giggled, then called me. "Come here, Ted. Come here and feel your daddy's muscles." Dad made a muscle and lifted me up with one arm, then he put me down and kissed me on top of my head. It was about noon then, and we'd just finished a late Sunday breakfast. I can still see him as he winked at my mom, the way he always did when they had a secret. He knelt down and put his hands on my shoulders.

"Want to go out for a ride?" he asked. "Just the two of us. Just the men."

"Yeah!" I yelled and started to jump up and down. I loved going driving with my dad. He'd put the top down no matter how cold it was, and we'd go out to the beltway and speed. I grabbed my Giants hat and a jacket and ran to my room to get ready. The car we had then was a 1956 Thunderbird. It was two years old but a beauty, and Dad kept it in tip-top shape. We washed and vacuumed it every other weekend and polished it with Turtle Wax three times a year—summer, fall, and spring. In the winter Dad wouldn't even drive it because of the snow and salt on the roads. He locked it in a garage and started it once a week to keep the fluids moving and the battery alive. Mom said we couldn't afford the car or the garage, but she loved it as much as he did, I think, and was just as happy that we had it.

I got ready first and waited outside for my dad. I walked around the T-Bird and looked at it. I knew I wasn't supposed to get in. That was one of Dad's rules for keeping it looking new. I couldn't eat or drink in the car because if I spilled, it would ruin the interior. I couldn't touch the windows because my hands left grease marks that were hard to remove. And never, ever, under any circumstances could I sit on the car or lean against it or rest packages or school books or keys or baseball gloves or anything else on the fenders, hood, or trunk because the paint could easily scratch or chip. So I sat down on the grass and waited a few feet from the car with my jacket and hat in my lap and listened as the door opened and watched him as he kissed my mom goodbye and came down the stairs with a smile. "How's my baby?" he said, running his hand along the black canvas top of the car. He always did that when he took the T-Bird out for a ride. He called the car his baby, Mom was his babe, and I was his big sonny boy.

He unlocked his door and opened mine, and together we unfastened the top and lowered it, making sure it didn't catch or crimp as we folded it down. Then he took one side and I took the other and we snapped the red cover down over the top. It was a warm autumn day and sunny, a perfect day for a drive. I got into the car and sat next to the window, where Mom usually sat, and watched Dad as he walked around and examined the tires.

"Are you ready?" he finally asked. I nodded. He reached over and locked my door. Then he turned the key and smiled again as the engine caught and went Vrooom. While the car warmed up, Dad put on his mirrored sunglasses, the type that you can't see a person's eyes through. He took a cigarette from a pack of Camels, tapped it on the back of his hand, and placed it between his lips. Then he twisted the rearview mirror so he could see himself, and he took out his comb and began combing his hair. When he was done and the engine was warm, he put the mirror back in place, lit his cigarette, and inhaled. I always thought of him as my dad, but I think he saw himself as a young Bogie or Frank Sinatra. He blew out the smoke and reached over and rubbed my head. "Let's go get 'em," he said, "you and me," and he slid the T-Bird into reverse.

We headed out towards the beltway. It was a beautiful day, clear and dry, with a warm wind blowing in our faces. I had to hold onto my cap. We had the radio on and we were singing along with the music. In the distance, I saw the sign for our cutoff. Dad saw it too, and he pushed his foot down on the accelerator. The car picked up speed with ease. We must have been doing seventy, seventy-five miles an hour. We turned the radio up and the heat on and sang louder. It seemed like we were the only car on the road. "Hey," Dad yelled, so I could hear him over the wind and the radio, "do you know what today is?"

I shook my head yes and said, "Sunday."

Dad laughed. "That's right, my big sonny boy, it's *Son*-Day...." and I giggled because I got it: "It's a day for fathers and sons." Then he put his arm around me and squeezed.

We were moving along at over eighty now and heading out toward the beach, where the traffic was thinner and we could safely speed. "See that car way up there?" Dad pointed. "See how far away it is?" I nodded. "Count and see how long it takes to pass him." I started counting, and in no time at all, maybe twelve seconds, we moved past him like he was standing still. "Get a horse," Dad yelled, and we laughed and waved our arms and howled into the wind as the speedometer needle moved past 90.

We drove on like that for a while, until the road became straight and empty—a perfect place to let go. Dad accelerated and pushed the car close to 100, then over 100. The speedometer itself went up to 120. The fastest I'd ever gone was 110. We were now at 103. We were flying. That's what it felt like—flying. The radio was on full blast and I could barely hear it. We were moving so fast I could hardly see. There was just us and the wind and the car and the road. Dad pushed it. 107...110...112...-13...-14....The car shook—Dad hesitated. I could feel him lift his foot from the pedal. "Are you scared?" he yelled. "No," I said, and seeing he couldn't hear me, I shook my head and shouted, "No, not a bit."

Dad nodded and pushed his foot down and the T-Bird surged ahead....113, -14, -15, -17, -19. At 120 the needle hovered. It held there. Lingered. We watched it, we waited—and when it finally crossed the mark we hollered and yelled, "We did it! We did it! We did it!" Then Dad took his foot off the pedal and let the car slow down to sixty. It felt like we were standing still. At the next cutoff he turned around and we headed home.

On the ride back one of us would occasionally say something about "Breaking the limit" or "Crossing the barrier," but most of the time we were quiet. We were exhilarated, full of ourselves and what we accomplished. We felt brave and strong like ancient gods and conquering heroes. We had been tested and we passed the test. Down the road, way ahead, I saw the car we had passed earlier. We drove past it again and waved. The guy waved back, then pulled ahead of us, and with no warning at all cut us off. Dad jammed on the brakes and turned the wheel hard to avoid hitting him. I hit my head on the dash. "You ok?" Dad asked, "You ok?" and he reached over and touched my head. It hurt a little—there was a small bump already, I could feel it—but I wasn't really hurt and I told him so. "Yes," I nodded, "I'm ok." "Shit," Dad cursed. "That asshole. The stupid son of a bitch." Then he peeled out and pulled even with the guy and stared at him for a long time and called him a jerk. The guy stared back, then dropped behind us. Sitting next to him, I saw, was a kid.

We drove on like that for a while, keeping an eye on him and then forgetting him until we finally came to our exit. We turned off. The guy followed, and as we stopped at a stop sign, he pulled around us and blocked the car. Dad and I watched as he got out of his car—a rusty and dented old Chevy—and stood by his open door. He was older than my dad, in his thirties, and shorter and wiry-looking. He was wearing pressed dungarees, a Yankees cap, and a white T-shirt, and he hadn't shaved in a couple of days. He lifted his cap and ran his fingers through his hair, then walked around to the back of his car and put his hands on the T-Bird's hood. Dad looked at me and got out of the car. "Who the fuck do you think you are?" the guy started screaming. "What the fuck are you doing? Where the fuck are you going?" Dad tried to calm him down, but the guy got louder and louder. Each time he said something, he pushed down hard on the car and made it bounce. Dad was talking too, but I couldn't hear him. Finally, the guy slapped the hood of the T-Bird with his palm and walked away.

Dad got back in the car, furious, cursing, calling the guy crazy, an idiot, nuts, a moron, and wrote down his license plate number as soon as the guy drove away. I watched as Dad wrote, watched his fingers, watched his hand, his writing, the way the numbers and letters came out broken and bent, tore through the paper, and went way outside of the lines, and I looked at his face and I saw it, and I'll never forget it, though I never saw it that way again. He was scared. Really scared. Frightened.... My dad was frightened. The same way I was of the night, the dark, of going to sleep and being attacked by ghosts. Scared white. Scared green. Scared red. Scared silly. Scared so bad he turned to me and said, "Guess we showed him, huh, big fella!"

I nodded.

"Sometimes, you know, it's smarter to walk away."

I turned away, then heard a slap and turned back and saw Dad punching his fist into his palm. "Sure would have liked to have belted him, though. Were you scared?"

"Uh-uh," I shook my head.

"No? Not just a little?

"Uh-uh."

"What if I'd hit him and he pulled a knife?"

"I'd have hit him hard, in the head, with a rock."

We looked at each other then and we broke out laughing because each of us knew we were lying. Dad reached out and touched my head, kissed the bump, and held me. "Let's not tell Mom how this happened," he said.

I looked at him, surprised. "How come?"

"She'll only worry about us next time we go out. She'll think when we go places we fight."

So I never did. I never told my mother or my sister or my wife—or anyone else all these years. It's a secret I've kept for my dad. And the truth is, I hardly ever recall it. It's something that hardly matters at all, except at certain times and places like at Grand Central Station, when I'm standing with my son and I'm afraid that someone will say something or do something or something will happen and I won't be able to pretend that it didn't, and I'll have to act, and I'll be petrified, and I wonder: Is this the day I fall from grace?

A Modern Myth

I wake up early, unable to sleep any longer, bothered by something I think I know. For a while I lie there and watch the numbers as they first appear then disappear on the digital clock that sits on the antique table next to the bed. Then I roll over and put my arm around Emily, my wife. She moans: of contentment, surety, comfort. I squeeze her gently and pull her closer, and she, having slept like this for twenty-two years, nuzzles in. I have been dreaming again about Simone: Simone crossing and uncrossing her legs, turning the pages of her book, lighting a cigarette, inhaling, exhaling, sipping a café au lait, doing the most ordinary of things, Simone. Lying there, arm around Emily, listening to the numbers in the clock click forward, I cannot escape Simone's constant beauty. I pull Emily closer and breathe deeply the familiar smell of her hair. I kiss her shoulder, her back, her neck. I love her so very much.

Down the hallway I hear a noise. Bill Jr.? I listen. The toilet flushes. A door squeaks. I can't sleep anyhow, so I get up to see what's what. It's Jane. In nothing but a tee shirt. "Oh, Mr. Wells," she whispers, "did I wake you?" I can barely talk. I can't talk. Her beauty leaves me breathless. I shake my head, no, nope, uh-uh. I become an idiot, a stumbling, bumbling idiot. Then I wave. Wave! It's five-thirty in the morning, I'm forty-seven years old, standing in the hallway of my own house, holding a robe tightly tucked around me like a frightened old house frau, and waving like an idiot to my son's girlfriend.

"Good night," she smiles. "See you later. On the beach. At the picnic." The picnic. Emily's idea. As an icebreaker. This icebreaker is melting my heart.

I continue on down the hallway and down the stairs to make a pot of coffee. The paper, I see, is already here, on the front lawn getting soaked by the early autumn dew. I go out and get it and bring it in with me to the kitchen. Then, when the coffee is brewed, I take a cup and the paper and settle down on the living-room couch. I try to read, but all I can think about is the picnic and Jane and the beach, and I wonder: how in God's name will I keep from making an old goat of myself if she shows up wearing a bikini?

By the time Emily wakes up, I have dressed and gone out for sweet rolls and am settled into the paper. I have a fire going in the fireplace and the *Brandenburg* playing softly. I look up when I hear her coming down the stairs and see her feet, her calves, her knees, see that she's wearing the sexy robe I bought her for her birthday five or six or seven years ago, and all of it, suddenly—Jane, the beach, Simone, Bill Jr., Emily, the robe—makes me feel very ordinary and embarrassed and afraid.

Emily smiles and walks into the kitchen. She comes back with a cup of coffee and a Danish, kisses me on top of the head, and sits down on the carpet beside my legs, resting her back against the couch. "Not the kind of day for a picnic," I tell her. "Too cold and windy and wet."

She nods and turns towards me. I see that she has already showered and put on lipstick. "It's still early," she says, and twists and kisses my leg. Beneath her robe I see the lace of her black silk teddy being pushed by the curve of her breast. I lean over, crumpling the paper in my lap, and kiss her on her mouth.

"Mmmmmmm," she smiles, "that's nice." Upstairs, a door opens.

Emily sits up and looks at me with her big eyes.

"Bill Jr. and Jane," I tell her.

She frowns and straightens her robe. "They were supposed to stay at her place. The plan was to pick them up there and then go out on a picnic." A door closes, and we listen together, Emily and I: to silence, then giggles, then silence.

"What do you think he's doing?" I finally ask.

"Probably exactly what you'd like to do," she says, then picks up my hand and kisses it.

Upstairs, the bed squeaks. It bangs against the wall again and again. Someone moans–my son, Willy-Billy?–and in the space of time between one sound and another, I wonder what can it be like to be inside of her, on top of her, to feel her move, see her face, touch her hair, smell her. What is it like to be intimate, part and parcel of such perfect beauty? I imagine lying down with Helen, Cleopatra, Aphrodite, Elizabeth Taylor in *Giant*, Jane. Emily pulls me. I beg off. "C'mon, Em, we can't do it now. The kids." She lets go of my hand and glares.

"I thought you would have wanted to," she says. "You dreamt about Simone."

Everything is quiet after that. Emily is in the kitchen finishing the crossword, and I'm lying on the couch with the paper strewn all around me. I don't know why she does that, Emily, about Simone. I don't even know what it means to her when she brings her up. Me, though, it leaves feeling foolish and angry. I'm sorry that I ever told her the truth. I sit up and pick up the paper. I look at the headlines. I look at the pictures. My eyes follow the shapes of the print, but the truth of the matter is I have no idea what's happening. I'm reasonably comfortable, in love with my wife, and proud of my son, and I sometimes think I'd throw it all away if his girlfriend so much as gave me a nod. If she ever touched me or brushed against me, who knows what I'd do. I'd probably give her half my portfolio.

"Wow!" Emily shrieks as she enters the living room from the kitchen. "I know that music. I *do*." I know what she's doing. I shake my head in disdain. "That's like a *movie* theme."

"C'mon, Em," I say. "Quit it."

"Oh, what is it? I know it. I just saw it too, the other night on the VCR. Oh, it was so good. Like about ESP and time tripping. You know, I know you know. Oh, oh, what is it. C'mon, C'mon, C'mon.

"It's Bach."

"Bach?"

"Ok, it's Pablo Casals playing Bach. The *Brandenburg Concerto.* Number four."

"Radical," Emily says, and throws her arms around me. She knocks me over and falls on top of me, pinning me down, giggling, and saying over and over, "I love you, Willy Billy Billy Willy, I do, I do, I swear I do, forever." Then she rolls off of me and bursts out laughing hysterically. "God," she says, pausing between bursts, trying to catch her breath, "God...I'm glad...I'm not...nineteen...again...." I shake my head. This is a game Emily recently started to play. She calls it Young Loins. She began it one night after hearing Bill Jr. and Jane professing their love and Jane calling him Willy Billy. Since then we've played it irregularly, and each time it has ended the same: with Emily saying "God, I'm glad I'm not nineteen again," and me just shaking my head.

I stand up and walk to the window. The sun is trying to come out. "So what do you want to do today?" I ask. There's no way I'm going to a picnic–at the beach–with Jane. Emily comes over to me and puts her arm around my hips. She looks at the sky, the trees, the grass, at me. "I don't care," she says. "The picnic was my idea, you decide. I'm going upstairs to get dressed."

Now what? I don't know. There's really nothing I want to do but pull the covers over my head and hide out. I run up the stairs and into our bedroom. Emily is in the bathroom, wearing only her teddy, standing sideways in front of the mirror. "Em," I call, and she jumps and reaches for her robe."How about a VCR sort of day?" She looks at me all big eyes and smiles. "Sure," she says, as she slides her arms into the robe and belts herself up, "whatever."

I go back down the stairs and get my jacket, put it on, and go back up. "Time to get up," I yell, knocking twice on Bill Jr.'s door as I walk past. "I am up, Dad," Willy Billy calls out, and he and Jane start to giggle. I stop in my tracks: does he think I don't get it? Does he care? Has he any idea, any notion at all, that whatever it is he and Jane are doing in there—or have done or will do—that his mother and I and zillions of others have already done and have been doing for several thousand millennia?

"Em," I call, sticking my head into the bedroom. She sticks hers out from the bathroom. "Why don't you tell the kids to plan their own day. We can hook up with them later this evening for dinner."

"Ok," she nods, and disappears back into the bathroom.

"Oh, Em," I call again, "any preference on the movies?"

"Nope," she calls. "It's up to you."

An hour and a half later I come back with two bags of deli groceries and three early Brando films. I turn onto our street and scan the cars in front of the house and see, as I hoped, that Jane and Bill Jr. are gone. I pull into the driveway and head for the side door that leads to the kitchen. I want to put everything away so that I can surprise Emily later when we're alone. I open the door slowly, close it quietly, and tiptoe in.

"Hi," Jane says. I nearly trip over myself as I look for her. Then I see her. She is kneeling down, near the refrigerator, wiping the floor, wearing a red tank top and a tight pair of jeans. "I spilled," she says.

I smile. I can barely look at her. She goes back to wiping. I can't take my eyes off her. Her waist–my God–it's so tiny I'm sure I could stretch my hands around it. I put the bags down on the counter and start putting things away. "I thought you had left," I finally manage to say. "I didn't see your car in the driveway." She looks up at me and brushes her hair from her eyes. "Bill took it. He's filling it up and checking the oil and water and tires."

I nod. She stands and walks over to where I am. I know she is moving at normal speed, but it seems to me like stop-frame slow-motion action. She reaches into the bag I have my hand in and begins to take things out. I step back and lean forward. With all my might I'm trying not to brush against her, touch her, look at her, smell her. I just want to empty that bag. Her fingers touch mine. My heart jumps. "Sorry," she says, and smiles. I just want to be twenty-one again and make love all night and know what I know now. I want another shot at Simone. I hear the front door. "Bill!" I call, "In the kitchen! We're in here!" He walks in all grins and smiles, sees Jane, and goes over to where she's standing and drapes his arm over her shoulders and around her neck as if that's the most natural place for it to be. I look at him, my son, Bill Jr., and I wonder what it is exactly Jane sees. I flatter myself and say *me*. She sees me when I was nineteen.

Emily comes into the kitchen. I put my arm out, and she walks right into its arc. I pull her close to me, and together Bill Jr. and Jane and Emily and I stand there looking at each other. Only they look at us as if we're invisible, and I look at them amazed.

"So what are you kids going to do today?" Emily asks. She is directing her question to Bill. I'm watching Jane. She reaches into his jacket pocket and takes out a pair of Jackie-O-hiding-from-paparazzi sunglasses.

"We're going to the beach," she says, looking up at Bill Jr. and kissing him on the cheek. It's obvious they've talked about this already and that he wants to do something else. She brushes back her hair and puts on the glasses, and for a second there I envy her and hate her for the ease with which she will always get what she wants.

"Ok," he says, "if you want." Then he comes over and shakes my hand. "See you later, Dad." He kisses his mother good-bye.

Jane walks over and hugs Emily. She looks at me, takes one step forward and stops. I have already turned away and am reaching into the cabinet behind me for a glass. "Be careful," I call over my shoulder.

"Look at this," I keep saying to Emily. "Will you look at this?" We are watching *Streetcar.* Blanche has already arrived. Brando walks into the apartment. He takes off his cap and jacket. His hair is all tousled. He's sweaty. You can see that he is actually small in stature, not a very big man at all. Sometimes his voice even sounds strange, slightly off. But his potency, his strength, the virility. It gives *me* goose bumps just to see him. Emily, though, is hardly watching. She is walking in and out of the room, picking up this, putting away that, sitting for a moment, then going off to do something else. "God, Em, sit *down* and look at this."

She comes over and sits on the bed with me. We watch for a while, and I continue ooohing and aaahing about Brando. "Vivien Leigh looks good, doesn't she?" Emily says. I look at her as if she is as looney as Blanche. Vivien Leigh looks awful: gaunt, wispy, frail, as if she really is disintegrating from the inside out. I don't know what to say, so I don't. I just continue to watch. Emily gets up and walks towards the bathroom. She stops in the doorway, turns around, and says, "Brando's a fat pig now. Do you know that? He weighs over three hundred pounds." Then she disappears into the bathroom.

"So what," I call to her. "It doesn't matter. He's a classic, a modern myth. He'll be like this forever—just like Liz will always be Liz and Marilyn will always be Marilyn."

"That's just wonderful," Emily says, sticking her head out from the bathroom, "just great. But in the real world they are all fat or old or dead." She disappears again, and I go back to Brando. "And do you know what else?" she calls. "Right now, today, at this very moment, Simone is older and fatter than me."

I get up and go into the bathroom. Emily has her hands on the sink and is leaning forward looking into the mirror. I walk up behind her and circle her with my arms. "Em?" She lowers her head. "I never even spoke with her, I told you that. It was twenty-five years ago in Paris. I was a student. I saw her once. In a café, drinking coffee. I don't even know her real name." Emily nods. "She's a fabrication. You know that. A dream, just a picture of something beautiful that I once saw, sat across from, stared at, and happen—who knows why—to still fantasize about in my dreams. I was too chicken to even say *bon soir*. I feel like a coot, a stupid old fool, every time you bring her up."

"How do you think *I* feel," she says? I flinch. I have no idea. "To you she's always twenty, young, and beautiful, and I am forty-two. It's hard enough with Jane around all the time. Sometimes it's just too much." I turn her around to face me. Her eyes are red and puffy. I kiss her. I hug her. I lick the trail of tears from her eyes, her cheek, down her neck. I go with her, hand in hand, back into the bedroom, to our bed.

Later, when we are lying in bed quietly, with the deli food all around us and my arm over Emily's belly, I say to her, "Jane is so beautiful she frightens me." "I know," Emily says. "She reminds me of Simone," I whisper. "I know," Emily says again. I lift myself up on my elbow and look at her. "What *don't* you know?" I ask. She smiles. "I don't know why *women* are thought of as romantics and *men* as down-to-earth." Then she laughs and touches my chest. I lower my head and kiss her breast, her nipple, her mouth, her eyelids. I am amazed at how lucky I am that she loves me.

At seven o'clock Emily nudges me. I am groggy, tired from wine and love. I open my eyes. She is already up and dressed. "Time," she says. I close my eyes. "Come on now, Bill Jr. and Jane are expecting us. We told them we'd have dinner together tonight."

I open my eyes. "Are they back yet?" I ask, and as soon as I do, I hear their laughter from downstairs and feel the vibrations of the turned-up bass. "They're here," I moan, and sit up. Emily pulls me out of bed.

The music becomes louder as we walk down the stairs. I lean over the railing and look into the dining room. Bill Jr. and Jane are dancing. Emily pokes me in the ribs and smiles. I smile back and continue to watch them. I can't believe how Jane moves. I can't believe *anyone* can move like that—and I thank my lucky stars that Emily and I never had a girl. "Hi," Bill calls, and waves. Jane stops moving in mid-thrust. She lowers her arms and quickly goes over to his side. "We brought a pizza back," she says, "and some beer and chocolate-chip ice cream."

"Good," I say. "Let's eat."

During the meal I manage to refrain from looking at Jane. I'm afraid if I do my face will break—or I'll sigh an audible sigh. But now we are all in the kitchen saying our good nights, and I am facing her. I can hardly bear her beauty. I wonder, my God, how can she? Still, I can't help myself. I stare. She catches me and looks back. She pushes the hair from her face and smiles. I lower my eyes. Then I look at Emily, who I've loved now for more than one hundred seasons, and at Bill Jr., who has somehow become a man. I look back at Jane. She is laughing, teasing Bill and resisting him as he pulls her towards the door. "There's no rush," she says. "We've got plenty of time." Then she walks over to Emily and hugs her and kisses her good night. I watch her. She looks at me, smiling, filled-up-brimming, full of herself and her day. She has no idea what's coming. She has no idea what's next. She steps forward and gives me a hug.

Her Mother, She Knows, Won't Like Him

Sara is the first person to arrive at work, as usual. She unlocks the office door and turns on the lights. The phone rings. Sara knows it's her mother so she lets it ring on. She hangs her jacket up, puts her purse in her file drawer, makes herself comfortable, then picks up the phone. "Hi, Mom."

"Sonja met someone and gave him your number." Sara winces but refuses to bite.

"She told him to call you at work."

"Mo-ther!"

"I didn't do it, my sister did. She says he's very nice."

"And how would she know?"

"She's been married to Lou for thirty-five years, that's how."

"Then how would you!" That, Sara thinks, ought to get her. At Sara's age her mother had three kids, two ex-husbands, and a live-in lover. So what could she say? She left Sara's father for her first lover when Sara was six—and after him there were a dozen more. "Bad dates," her mother calls them. She says it without rancor now, or surprise, as if what she's talking about is rotten fruit.

Her mother sighs into the phone. It's her "I'm Only Trying To Do What's Right Why Am I So Misunderstood" sigh. It's a sound Sara's heard all her life. She does it again, louder, and says, "I'm sorry. I just thought it would be good for you to meet a *nice* man for a change. Easier, I mean. I should know."

What a joke! Sara closes her eyes and shakes her head. All her life her mother's told her, "Men are easy. They only want one thing," and now here she is, setting Sara up. "Maybe we can double," Sara says sarcastically. She's thirty-three, her mother's fifty, and both of them are still looking for love.

Her mother doesn't answer her. Sara puts her glasses on and absently begins turning the pages of her desk calendar forward. She sees "Mother's Birthday Dinner" tomorrow night and "Eye Exam" and "Gloria's Party" next week. She starts to flip the pages backwards and stops. She doesn't want to get even close to where she knows written in red is "RJ Downstairs at Mario's," the place Ray Johnson finally admitted he was married. Now Sara doesn't know what to do. Her mother goes out with jerks all the time. For someone else, though, *For Sara,* and with Sonja's help, who knows, maybe, just maybe.... Stranger things than this happen in life.

"All right, Mom," Sara sighs, "I'll do it, but you tell Sonja he has to call between ten and ten-fifteen while everyone's on their break."

"That's what I told her, between ten and ten-fifteen. His name's Richard Evans and..." She tells Sara all about him.

Ever since then, Sara's been edgy. She can't concentrate on what she's doing and isn't interested in the office banter. All morning she's been dreaming and making mistakes. She makes another, hits the wrong key and wipes out a paragraph. She glares at the screen, at the big empty space she's created, then puts her glasses on and looks through the glass-paneled doors and sees the numbers above the elevator rising. Let it be a sign that her life's about to pick up. She looks at the clock. It's ten-ten. He's not going to call, she knows it. She's going to be stood up by someone who's never even met her. "Thanks, Mom," she mutters, and as soon as she does, the phone rings.

Sara stares at it. She's no longer sure if she wants it to be him or not. She counts the rings, half hoping they'll stop, and when they don't and there's nothing else she can do, she lifts the phone hesitantly and says, "Warden, Hickle, and Hickle." And waits....

"Sara?" she hears.

"Yes."

"This is Richard," and right away, as he continues to speak, when she hears the softness in his voice, which is almost southern, but isn't, is midwestern, she's curious. He has her laughing and talking in no time, and he seems to be really nice, and that—plus what her mother's told her—has Sara interested. Meanwhile, she's watching the clock. It's almost ten-fifteen and he hasn't asked her out. She's not sure what she should do. She doesn't want to push him, but she doesn't want to be on the phone with him either when Lois, Ginger, and Jeanne return from their breaks. He begins telling her about her mother and Sonja and how they all met, but Sara doesn't want to hear about that, she wants to go out with him. "So, when do you think *we* should meet?" she says.

He's surprised, she can tell, but he laughs and answers, "Anytime. How about tonight? It's Friday. Dinner and a show. Are you free?"

Sara looks at her calendar and smiles. "Yes," she says, "I am," and she gives him her address and adds her phone number, "In case something happens and you can't make it." Then she hangs up the phone elated, certain she's done the right thing until she remembers her last two dates were disasters.

The first guy, Rob, actually set her up with his friend, and the second guy, a guy she really fell for, left her stranded at a party and went home early with somebody else. She feels sick. She hasn't even met him yet, and already she's blown it: she shouldn't have asked him out; she shouldn't have cut him off; she should have said she was busy; she should have been harder to get. Sara picks up the phone to call Gloria, but with each number she pushes she feels better—he really could be the one.

No luck. Gloria is out, running an errand for her boss, and her mother's line is busy. Sara hangs up the phone and begins to think about Richard. He's tall, her mother said, fair, blond and blue-eyed, short-haired, clean-shaven, and well-dressed. He works for the City as a social worker, has never been married, and has a master's degree from Notre Dame. He's definitely a man her mother would like.

Her face begins to smile, Sara can feel it. No one she's gone with has ever been smarter than she *and* someone her mother would like. She stops herself. They haven't even met and already she's thinking about going with him. That's dumb—and it's dangerous. He could be a jerk, and she might not *really* like him. *He* might not like *her*. Her stomach knots. What if he asks her about the show they see, and she doesn't understand it or has nothing of interest to say? With Ray that was never a problem. He only took her to dives where all they ate was fried chicken, pizza, or hamburgers, and he always did all of the talking, about Magic's latest dunk or his lousy job, and she didn't have to do a thing. She feels nauseous. Her head aches. Why would Richard be interested in her? She picks up the phone to call Sonja.

"Sara, what's wrong?"

She looks up. It's Lois. Perfect, as always—her clothes, demeanor, tone, her timing.

"I'm going out," Sara says. "Tonight."

"Oh, Sara, that's wonderful."

"Yeah."

"Come on now." Lois is shimmering. It's as if this is her evening instead of Sara's. "Don't do this to yourself." Ever since Ray dumped Sara, Lois has been urging her to get out and meet different people. She even set her up with a friend of her husband's, but that didn't quite work out. He was separated from his wife and very, very nice and available, and he wanted to see her again, but after two hours Sara knew she wasn't interested. He was just too solicitous and wishy-washy.

"Jeanne. Ginger. Sara's met someone."

Sara blushes, she can feel it. She's embarrassed by this fuss Lois is making for what seems so commonplace for everyone else. It reminds her of her retarded cousin, Patsy, and the way everyone applauds when she ties her shoes.

"Who is he?" Jeanne asks.

"A friend of a friend," Sara whispers.

"Does your mother know?"

She nods.

"Is he–you know, *special*?"

Sara takes off her glasses. The reason she hasn't been going out, she's told them, is that she's looking for someone special–a man with brawn *and* a heart. "I don't know," she says, "I haven't met him yet. He's really nice, though. And smart!"

"Ooow, Sara..." They sing in glee. They're all married, have been for years, as long as they've been with Warden, Hickle, and Hickle, and they all want the same for her, want Sara to join their club. And she wants it too, more than anything.

"What are you doing?" Ginger asks. "What'll you wear?"

"Oh God! Everything I like is at the cleaners and won't be back for a couple of days."

"Take the afternoon off," Lois says. "Take care of yourself. Get your hair done. Buy some new clothes. Put on a different face." Lois is telling her what she would do.

Sara shakes her head. "I can't. Not today."

"Sure you can. You've got sick days. You have personal leave. You can take a day, a half-day...." Jeanne and Ginger nod their heads in approval. "Don't go rushing home. Take your time. Be good to yourself. Do it slow!"

"I *can't*. Henry has to have this transcript today. I promised him."

"How long will it take you?"

"I don't know." She looks at her watch. "If I don't have lunch I could probably finish by two or two-thirty."

"Good," Jeanne claps, "I'll call my sister, Marge. She's not working today, but she can set an appointment for your hair at three. We'll cover anything that comes up after that. Ok, girls?" They all nod. "Ok."

Sara agrees, and for the next two and a half hours she sits at her computer and types and types and types and types and hardly makes any mistakes. She stops only to eat a carrot that Lois brings her back from her lunch, then returns to her typing renewed. At a quarter after two she finishes.

"That's it. I'm done. Typed and proofed." She's pleased with herself and her work. She slides the transcript to the center of her desk. On top of it she writes a note. "Went home early. Have a headache...." She stops. It isn't necessary to lie. Henry Hickle is a kind and decent man. She tears up the note and begins again. "Went home early. Had some personal business to attend to. Will be back on Monday, as usual." Then she signs her name and sits there, stalling for a moment or two.

Lois, Ginger, and Jeanne are busy typing. They don't bother to look up when Sara stands to get her purse. She opens her filing cabinet drawer and reaches in. Covering her purse is a Macy's bag. Inside the bag is a gift-wrapped box. Sara turns around. Lois, Ginger, and Jeanne are standing and smiling.

"Open it," says Lois.

"It's you," points Ginger.

Carefully, as at Christmas or her birthday, Sara peels the wrapping paper just the way her mother taught her and folds it back gently to save it. With her fingernail she snips the tape and opens the box. "Oh, it's beautiful!" she says, dropping the wrapping paper to the floor and holding up the black silk blouse.

"Do you like it?"

"I love it. It's perfect. It's so simple and soft and delicate. You shouldn't have."

"Consider it an early birthday present."

"Or a late one."

Then Lois, Ginger, and Jeanne gather around Sara and hug her, each of them wishing her a very special time. Sara feels like she's going to cry. The gift is more than a gesture. It is tenderness. She loves these women with whom she works.

"Hurry now," Jeanne says, "or you'll be late for your appointment. Don't worry. Everything here is under control."

They walk her out to the elevator, laughing and giggling, and when it finally arrives and the doors open, they hug her again and begin waving goodbye. Sara smiles and waves back at them, holding the Macy's box close to her chest. For the first time in weeks she's ecstatic. She can feel her smile all over her face.

In the lobby she stops to go to the women's room to freshen up. It's empty, so she pauses at the mirror and looks at herself. She brushes back her hair with her hand and leans forward. She smiles, puckers, pouts, sticks out her tongue, and laughs. She doesn't look half bad, and with her new haircut she'll look even better. She puts on her glasses. They look terrible, and she remembers that she has an eye exam next week and makes a mental note to order a new pair of frames. Then she powders her nose, puts on fresh lipstick, and steps back to get a full-length view of herself. She stands there looking, taking her glasses off and putting them on. "Statuesque," she murmurs and winks, putting her hands on her hips and acting sultry until she hears the door open and leaves.

At the beauty shop she has to wait. She picks up an old *Romance* magazine and blindly leafs through the pages. If she has a good time tonight she'll invite him to Gloria's party–and then to her family's annual Memorial Day cookout. It would be the first time ever that she brought a man her mother would like. Maybe even by then she can get him to grow a beard or a mustache. Sara likes that. Hair on the face is a turn on.

"Sara?" a man calls.

"Yes." She looks up.

"I'm Eric. Hmmmm. You're next."

She stands and follows him to the chair that's farthest from the front door. She's not at all sure if she likes him or should trust him—he's a strange little bird of a man. Everything on him moves as he speaks: his arms, hands, hair, his tunic. He's so wispy. She sits in his chair and waits.

"Well, what can we do to you today? Hmmm." He flutters.

"Just cut it back a little. Not too short in the front."

"Hmmmmm," he murmurs, placing his hand under her chin and lifting her head. "Hmmm," as he turns it left, then right. "Hmmm." He walks behind her and fluffs out her hair, turns her around and puts his hands on her cheeks. "Hmmmm Hmmmm."

"Is something wrong?"

"Well, with the shape of your face and the texture of your hair, I'd recommend a shorter cut, I would. Hmmmm. Yes."

Sara looks at herself in the mirror, trying to picture the look, and she can't. It's been years since her hair was cut short, and when it was, she always felt too exposed. She looks at the manicurist, Carol, who smiles, shakes her head yes as if in agreement, then shrugs her shoulder as if to say *I don't know, don't ask.*

"Ok, you're the expert. Let's do it." But for the next thirty-five minutes she refuses to look at herself in the mirror. All of her concentration goes to her shoes. She hears the scissors and feels the falling hair, but that's all. She won't look until Eric tells her to. Either she will be beautiful or a dump. Either way, Richard will have to accept her, because that's who she will be....

"Done!" Eric pronounces, and he spins her around and bows.

Sara is astounded. The short hair gives her a mysterious look: it makes her look unfathomable, like secrets and ghosts are buried deep in her eyes. "Oh my," she says. "It's fantastic."

"Yes," Eric says, "It is. Hmmmm." Then he walks all around her. "Now a little eye color.... A *Deep Shadow* and a lip gloss. Yes, that will do. You'll look ravenous. Hmmmmm. What are you doing tonight?" Sara smiles and pays the bill, also buying the eye shadow, nail polish, and lip gloss.

"You look fabulous," the shop owner says as he holds the door open for her. "Simply scrumptious."

Sara turns and walks down Grand. She's looking for a new pair of shoes. Half a block away, she sees a pair just like the pair she's wearing and buys them without even trying them on. She feels marvelous as she continues her walk, cutting down Seventh where there is a little less traffic and the stores are cheaper—in case she sees something else she wants.

At the corner she sees a skirt. She stops for a closer look and stares at her reflection in the window. She looks fine. Really fine—and with that new skirt, she'll be even finer. It'll go perfectly with her new blouse and shoes. Sara looks but can't see a price tag. She's certain it costs at least eighty dollars. She hesitates, pictures herself in the complete outfit, and decides not to buy it. She's already spent too much. Besides, it's getting late and she should be heading home if she's going to do it the way Lois said, taking care of herself and going slow. She sees herself reading a magazine when Richard arrives at her door. She turns and walks towards her car. Then she turns back. It *is* lovely. She *could* charge it—Richard will love how it looks. At least she should try it on.

Inside, the store is sedate. The saleswomen are conservatively dressed yet sleek. They are just the kind of women who usually overwhelm her with their surety. Usually, but not today. "Miss," Sara calls, "could I see that blue skirt in the window, the one with the buttons down the front, in a twelve?"

"It's back here," the saleswoman points, "follow me."

At the clothes rack Sara rubs the fabric between her fingers. She holds the skirt to the light to see the color and the length and unbuttons the top two buttons. It's the buttons that first attracted her attention. She thinks they are really sexy.

"It's on sale. Marked down from eighty-five dollars to forty-five. Would you like to try it on?"

"I really shouldn't."

"But you will anyway...." The saleswoman, Kris, laughs kindly. "I know because that's what I always say when I know I shouldn't, and I do."

Sara smiles at her and says, "Ok," and takes the skirt to the dressing room. She takes off her old skirt and buttons up the new one. The material feels good, light and airy and cool, almost as if it's not there. In the mirror she sees that it's the right length. It looks and fits as if it's hers. She loves it, but she wants another opinion. She puts her glasses on and goes out looking for Kris. On her way she passes a three-way mirror, stops, goes back, turns to the left, the right, all the way around, and looks at herself in the skirt....

"It's lovely," a man says. Sara turns around.

"Hi, I'm Jack. I'm the manager here." He's looking at Sara and smiling. She takes her glasses off and half smiles back. He has beefy shoulders, a neatly trimmed mustache, and dark wavy hair with touches of gray at his temples. He's wearing tan slacks, a dark blazer, and a pink shirt with the top two buttons undone. A gold bracelet hangs from his wrist.

"No kidding," he grins. "It's you. What's your name?"

"S-Sara," she says.

"Pleased to meet you," and he holds out his hand and takes hers. Then for the next few minutes he talks about the weather, the skirt she's wearing, this season's fashions. Sara begins to relax, and Jack, who has been watching her face all the time he's been talking, lowers his eyes and says, "I don't usually do this...." He's going to ask her out, she knows it...."But you look so fine...." He's really going to do it. "If you're not buying that skirt for someone special..."—Richard?— "and you don't have any plans for tonight..."—Richard!—"would you like to go out and get something to eat?" Richard.

Sara doesn't know whether to giggle or cry. *He* could be the one she's been looking for. She looks at his face. He is handsome. And she stares at his chest, which is hairy. "No," she says very slowly, "I'm not seeing anyone special...."

Jack nods as if that's the answer he expects.

"But I do have plans for tonight."

"That's too bad," he says.

"What about Sunday?" Sara asks with doubt in her voice.

"Can't," Jack shakes his head. "The store's closed and I won't be here. Some other time maybe," he smiles and walks away.

Sara watches him, admiring his gait and his torso. He moves with assurance, like somebody who usually gets what he wants. She feels terrible. There's not going to be any other time. He's never going to call her. He didn't even ask for her number.

Back in the dressing room, Sara looks at herself in the mirror. In her old blouse and shoes she looks dowdy and plain. She stares at her face. Her lipstick is faded and sad. No wonder Jack didn't ask for her number. Who could blame him? She begins to make herself up. She puts on her new shoes and blouse and feels better. She brushes on the eye shadow, the *Deep Shadow* that Eric recommended, and stares at herself, amazed: her eyes look hollow and deep—as if you could see down into her, all the way to the tips of her toes. She paints on the lip gloss and smiles her sexy smile at the mirror, which smiles it back. Then she unbuttons the top two buttons on her blouse and the bottom two buttons on the skirt and turns herself quickly around. She straightens the skirt and winks at herself in the mirror, and with her old clothes packed neatly away, heads out of the dressing room with a smile. She wants Jack to ask for her number.

He's at the front counter, tapping his finger on the glass. "You look fantastic," he says when she reaches him. Sara nods and smiles and laughs–and sneaks peeks at his hairy chest–and Jack continues to make small talk. Finally, he begins to work on her bill. "It really is too bad," he says keeping his eyes on the receipt, "that you have other plans for tonight. I think we could have had a good time."

Sara feels her whole body drop. He's not going to ask for her number. She watches his fingers as he writes. They're short and blunt, well manicured. "How about tomorrow night?" she sighs, knowing it's her mother's birthday dinner.

"I can't," he says.

Sara feels like she's going to cry. She looks over at Kris, who sees her and smiles. Kris would know what to do–and so would Lois. She looks back at Jack and sees Richard standing at her door and waiting. "I suppose," she says, "I *could* change my plans for tonight."

Jack looks at her and smiles.

"Yes, I'm sure I can."

"Let's go then," he says as he puts down his pen and walks around the counter to meet her. He takes hold of her arm and leads her towards the back door. "Lock up, will you, Kris," he calls out over his shoulder. Kris shakes her head and frowns. Sara wonders why and remembers that she hasn't yet paid for her skirt. She's about to say something and decides not to, not yet. She doesn't want to spoil the mood.

Outside, with her arm still in Jack's hand, Sara feels all tingly and goose-bumpy. It's been months since she's felt like this. She pulls his arm a little to get his attention. Jack nods and smiles a "Hi." Then he drops her arm and unlocks the car door; he holds the door open and lets Sara in. She watches him as he walks around the car, then reaches over and opens his door. "I know a little place downtown," he says. Sara leans back and looks out the window as Jack pulls away from the curb. She takes her glasses out of her purse and puts them on and looks at him–at his hair, his mustache, his hands–and relaxes.

During dinner she'll invite him to Gloria's party, and after that she'll bring him to her family's annual Memorial Day cookout. She reaches out and taps his hand. Jack turns and looks at her, he places his hand on top of hers, squeezes it a little, like a pump, and nods. Sara smiles. Her mother, she knows, won't like him.

Inside and Out

It's minus ten degrees Fahrenheit outside. With the wind-chill factor, it's minus thirty-four–it's too cold even for snow. But inside, just one story up and less than a foot away, it is summer twenty-four hours a day, the air is dry and sweetened, plants grow, flutes play, the drinks are served with ice. It's New Year's.

The living room here is painted ivory, the rugs are eggshell white. Glück plays on the stereo. The light, what little there is of it, flickers from candles and imitation Tiffany lamps, turning everything soft, like dusk. Throughout the room, like a jungle or an oasis, are palms, cacti, bonsai trees, succulents–in wicker baskets, on the floor, dangling from the ceiling, on tables, chairs, everywhere. And all around the plants, on bookshelves, the desk, the mantle, the walls, are dozens of black and white photographs, some over a century old, of nude and seminude women, alone and in groups, all of them consciously posing.

Two women are sitting in the middle of this room on a plush mauve couch that is soft and pillowed and curved. The younger woman, Amber, is seventeen and looks twenty-five. She takes her name from the color of her hair. The older woman is twenty-nine and looks twenty-one. Her name is Robyn. That's her real name, Robyn. Her working name is Kat. She's reading *Oui* and sucking an ice cube.

Amber leans against Robyn and slumps over, drunk. She giggles and twitches, then moans. She's reveling in dreams of love and family, a home, a yellow sports car, being an actress, an artist, the lead singer in a rock-and-roll band. She doesn't know—but she does really—that the only dream that will come close is family. She'll have two kids, both boys, from two different men, neither of whom will marry her or have anything to do with his offspring.

Robyn has a four-year-old boy and no man. She thinks she knows who the father is, but she wouldn't want to swear to it. She's been working here now for nine years. Most of that time, like tonight, she spends waiting. She has sat and waited for thousands and thousands of hours, and in that time and the time she spends recuperating from infection, surgery, and motherhood, Robyn reads, watches tv, drinks too much vodka, and thinks. She's read almost every *People, Psychology Today, Esquire, Redbook, Playboy, Oui, Vogue, Time, Life, Playgirl,* and Danielle Steel and Harold and Tom Robbins novel, and she's thought about things. She thinks about having it all, doesn't believe she'll ever get any of it, but really does, but doesn't, but does. Every year she thinks will be her last. Now she wants out by the time she's thirty. Amber wants out by eighteen....There's something Robyn has to say.

"Bad as it sometimes gets in here, it's good. You just have to remember that sometimes and remind yourself. And I'm not just talking about the money! Course, *that's* good, but so am I. But that's not the all of it, by a long shot. There's freedom. Yes, freedom! John buys less of me than your average hubby owns of his average wife. And I'm not plugged into anything either! The President couldn't find me if I didn't want him to. No jail record, no welfare, social security, or IRS. Don't even have a bank account. I pay all my expenses in cash and money order. Mail goes to a postal box, and the phone is in another name.

"I'll tell you something else, too. Plenty of times I like what I do—and it's not what some people might think either, some tv-movie-looking dude with smooth skin, muscles, sweet smells, and bucks. Uh-uh.

Those johns are one-in-a-trillion, and if they do come in, they're mean. Only reason they'd come here is to hurt you. The ones I'm talking about are different. Like the guy I had earlier with warts. Lots of girls wouldn't touch him, but that's what we're here for, baby, that's the *job*. Crystal wouldn't let them work here if they ever pulled that. Anyhow, there's plenty worse than warts. Ever seen burns? Those thalidomide flippers? Let me *tell* you.... Other thing is he's an old guy, seventy, seventy-five, and in a chair. I felt sorry for him, I did. It's the holiday season, he's in this raggedy-ass old chair, and probably has nowhere to go. I decide to be cheerful with him. 'What's your pleasure?' I say, soon as we get to the red room. 'Half and half? Round the world? What'll it be?' He doesn't answer. I've never seen him before, so I figure he's shy. I take off my nightgown and let him look. I turn around and around real slow so he can see whatever he can in the candlelight—and I touch myself, then I sit on his lap so he can touch me. His hands are real cold, hard and callused from the weather outside and the chair, but his touch is gentle and sweet. I let him touch me all over as much as he likes, where I don't let everyone go—but no kissing. When he's done and just holding me, I get off his lap and start rubbing him. 'Let's take him out and let him breathe,' I say, and that's when he tells me: 'I got warts.' I unbutton his pants, undo his zipper, reach into his undies, and take him out. I pull him, easy at first, then faster and harder till I locate his rhythm and he cums. I let him cum all over me. Honey, I don't know when I last saw a man so happy. Some folks would call this disgusting. To me it was beautiful. When I tucked him back away and zipped him in, he looked at me as if I was Our Lady of Lourdes herself."

She stops, cocks her head, listens to the sound of footsteps on the outer stairs, in the hallway, waits to hear if Crystal will open the inside door. The locks turn: one, two, three. She moistens her lips, splays her hair, cascades it over her shoulders. She puts another piece of ice in her mouth and chews it, tucks her left leg under her, pulls up her nightgown, and reveals a big piece of thigh. She does all of this automatically, as she has eight times earlier this evening and most evenings for the past nine years.

The inside door squeaks opens. She feels a rush of cold air cross her legs. Who will it be at two-thirty in the morning on New Year's Eve? Already she's had... She thinks back over her first eight, their fingers and hands, nails, lips, mouths, their teeth, and their smells. The door closes. She smiles, looks up, sees a skinny, blank-faced, eighteen- or nineteen-year-old blond boy. "Best in the house," she hears Crystal say. The boy looks over at Amber, who's passed out asleep on the couch. Robyn swallows what's left of her ice cube, stands, takes his hand, and leads him back to the red room, where she knows it's warm and a chilled bottle of Stoli is waiting.

She pours him a glass of vodka, then leads him to the queen-sized bed, where she sits down next to him and sips at her drink. "Want to tell me about it?" she says.

"I told her I was in the service–the Navy. I guess she could see that from the haircut. I told her how my girl in California dumped me and how my buddy set me up with a friend of his girl's for New Year's, but when they went off to their hotel, mine didn't want to, she wanted me to take her home. So I did, and my buddy told me I should come up here....

"All the while I'm talking, she's listening with her head on my chest. It's like she's listening to me inside and out–like sonar. My shirt is open–she unbuttoned it as soon as we sat on the bed. My pants are still on and we haven't done anything yet and I'm starting to feel pretty great. She gets up to get us another drink and I look at her really for the first time. It's like watching a movie, like she's really there but she's not. I would have gone for the other one, the blonde on the couch, if she hadn't have been blasted out, but I'm glad I didn't because this one was something else. She made me feel really great. I think she liked me. I *know* it's her job, but I think she did anyhow. It was like she really knew me. Could see me. And when she did me, let me tell you: she did me. She took me in her mouth and touched me softer than snow. I must have cum in less than thirty seconds. I spent two hundred and fifty on my buddy's girl's friend, and I felt like a zero. I spent seventy-five on Kat, and I feel like a king. I even gave her a thirty-dollar tip and my name, Jim Ryan, and told her I'd be back, and I will too, I mean it...."

"So how was he, honey?" Crystal asks, closing and locking the door behind him.

"Young. Eighteen. Nineteen. Navy."

"Hope he didn't want to prove himself with you, test his guns."

Robyn laughs. "No, mostly just talk, then a blow job."

"Why don't you hop in with me. I'm going to run a bath. Clean up and spend the night. It's New Year's and we could both use some loving."

"Not tonight, Crystal, I'm beat."

"You sure?"

"Yeah. I just need to sleep."

"Too bad," Crystal pouts. "It's nasty out there."

Robyn smiles, kisses Crystal on the cheek, the lips, almost reconsiders, then shakes her head. "Happy New Year, Crystal. See you tomorrow."

Crystal takes Robyn's hand and walks with her to the top of the rear stairs. She turns the light on and kisses her good night. Robyn hugs her and hurries down. She unlocks the heavy metal security door, yanks it open, and stops, face to face with her reflection in the storm door. She looks at herself filling in the glass like a picture—all bundled in her black leather coat with its bushy fox collar—and feels like one of those Russian princesses she's read about all her life. She smiles and ruffles her hair and imagines herself on the arm of her prince on the way to their dacha in the Crimea....

"Kat, you still there?" Crystal calls.

"Yeah. Just buttoning up. It's wicked out there." She raises her collar and looks at herself again and likes what she sees, how she looks, feels cozy-warm, earned-tired, rich. "Ok!" Crystal yells, and flips off the light and just like that, in a flick, Robyn's gone. She stands there looking out through the storm window and sees nothing but darkness and ice. She reaches out with her hand and touches the spot on the window where she was. She lets the chill of the glass slide up her arm, then turns away and slowly walks back up the stairs.

Crystal is in the bathroom, humming. The bath water is running and steam is seeping out through a crack in the bathroom door. Robyn walks over to the ice bucket, puts three cubes in a tumbler, covers them with vodka, and sits down on the couch next to Amber. She looks around her at the photographs of all the women, each perfectly framed, ensconced, unknown, and holds up her drink and salutes them. The ice crinkles, cracks, snaps. Robyn looks at her glass, she lifts it and holds it to her ear and listens, she listens as if the ice were talking to her, as if the world were inside and it was inviting her to come in and stay. Robyn puts her glass down and undresses, then she picks it up, walks to the bathroom, and pushes the door open with her toe. "It's me," she calls out as she steps into the mist.

Beginnings

1

The winter sun rose slowly, turning the sky from slate grey to indigo. The light–what little there was of it–snaked like the past through the present, through the tears in the curtains in her bedroom. Bernice, who had been watching, squeezed her eyes shut and massaged them. The curtains rustled. A shaft of cool air rushed over her face. She opened her eyes and saw the sun, which had been hiding behind a cloud bank, peek in over the windowsill, and settle on the night table on the other side of her bed. Behind her the Japanese print calendar rubbed against the wall. She tilted her head backwards: the pages of the months lifted themselves up.

"Yes," she whispered, "I know."

No.

2

He's dressed all in white–from shoes to shirt collar–and pulling at his black handlebar mustache. He's anxious. She smiles.... Good. Let him wait. Let him wonder.... She stands straight, remains still, delighting in the way she feels, the way she looks, the way her jade silk skirt brushes against her legs. She tips her hat–large-brimmed and ostrich-feathered–forward and walks across the street and kisses him from behind. He flusters. He stammers. He wipes the lipstick off his cheek.

For a moment he stares at her, but the lowered brim of her hat won't allow him to see what's there. He reaches for her hand. She gives it.... His hands are so much smaller than hers.... He holds tight to her index finger and gently, he propels her forward. "Where are we going?" she asks. "What's the rush?" He blushes and slows down, and says nothing until several minutes later when he stops in the middle of a street. "Here," he says shyly. "This is where I want to take you." She looks up. A peeling, mangled, cockeyed sign dangles above a doorway.... *Hôt de France...* She looks at him. He looks at her, then drops her hand and lowers his head, embarrassed. "I'm sorry, I thought you wanted to." She reaches out and touches his cheek, the one she kissed earlier, still marked red from her lips. He turns his face away. She pulls him back. "First I want to celebrate with a bottle of champagne. Then *Hôtel de France, j'arrive.*"

It was Paris. After the war. 1923. Bernice rolled over, wide awake. It was three o'clock in the morning, '...a real dark night of the soul...' Do I make myself clear?

No, probably not.

3

Try this. Bernice was excited. Having her family and friends over for dinner always made her nervous. Partly, she supposed, it had to do with her father, who was always fastidious about everything, but mostly, she knew it was Harold. She tried to remember everything he had told her. "Order the wine in advance. And don't forget the brandy, you always forget the brandy. Prepare for more people than are coming. How the meal looks is as important as how it tastes. Eyes are as vital as taste buds." Harold's little admonitions, his helpful hints, his advice—it was all he ever offered. "Think of the weather, Bernice, the temperature. People can't eat pot roast and gravy in the heat." Bernice thought about the weather—it was March, comfortably cool, and wet—and decided to make a bouillabaisse. "You can't make a bouillabaisse without rascasse," Harold told her. "It's the ugliest fish in the world. Genuine bouillabaisse can only be made in Nice." "Ok," she had said once, after one of his other suggestions. "If you know so much why don't you do it." "No, Bernice," he shook his head, "you do it better than I. I just know how to talk." Ah, but that was a long time ago, much too long ago to worry about now.... She decided to make fish fillets *bonne femme*.... Her little joke, which she was certain only Harold would get.... Sole fillets, she wrote down, followed by shallots, wine, heavy cream, chives, parsley, and mushrooms. Mushrooms, she underlined twice. Then she walked around the living room checking everything she knew Harold would check: liquor, glasses, the position of the chairs, the seating arrangement, the proper display of his rare collection of erotic Japanese etchings and books.... "Everything must be informal. The key is how it's arranged...." And, as she walked about, she added to her list everything else she would need. When she was finished, she put on her coat, stuffed the list in her pocket, and started to go out to the stores. "Bernice," Harold called, "remember to get some brie." She turned around and began to go over everything again.

Once more.

4

—Let's begin again. We can begin again.

—I don't know, Harold. I don't know.

—Sure we can. We can start over. Everything will change. I promise.

—Everything doesn't have to change. We don't have to start over. The beginning was fine; it was perfect. It's now—the middle—that stinks.

—Fine, good, Bernice. That's a start. Let's do the beginning again.... I love you.

—All right, Harold, we'll do the beginning again.

5

In the beginning Bernice didn't really care for Harold. He was too pompous: a *professeur de l'université*; too intelligent: a Mensa; too mystical: a Theosophist. He spoke to her for hours about past lives and reincarnation, telling her that he had been with Moses at the Red Sea, Jesus at Galilee, Caesar at the Rubicon, and Washington on the Delaware. "And," he said, "I still don't know how to swim."

"Next time come back as a bird," Bernice quipped. "That way you can fly over the water and look down on and judge the rest of us mere mortals."

"That's a great idea," Harold laughed. "I think I will. Birds are such cold-blooded beasts."

The next time she saw him he was different—shy and insecure. She had invited him to an opening-night performance, and afterwards to a party with the troupe. (Bernice was a dancer. She had come to Paris, where everyone was, to dance.) At first, Harold was in his milieu: talking about dance, music, and the theater. Later, though, when the musicians began to play and the dancers began to dance and the actors and actresses improvised, mimed, and generally began horsing around, Harold shrank. He went off to a corner and observed, and Bernice, who was the center of much attention, observed him. "Let's dance," she said, taking his hand and pulling him towards the music. Harold shook his head. "Too tired?" she mocked. "Or just bored?" Wanly, Harold smiled—actually more of a grimace. "I can't, Bernice. I don't know how." With anyone else she would have persisted, would have pulled him to the center of the floor insisting, but standing there alone in his corner, looking at his tiny feet—so forlorn, so beaten—Harold was the essence of pathos. Bernice slipped her arm through his and whispered into his ear, "Someday I'll teach you,"—which she did—"that and all kinds of other things as well. Now, put your arm around me and take me to the *Dôme*."

Four weeks later they are standing in front of the *Hôtel de France,* and eight months after that they are married. Their first twenty years are *bon temps.* Is that a good beginning?

Perhaps.

6

"Happy anniversary, Bernice," says Charles.

"And Harold Harvey too!" adds Martine, raising her glass to the skylight.

"How many years has it been?"

Bernice looks at Donald and smiles.

"Donald never remembers such things," pouts Charles, looking directly at Donald and mock-scowling. "The only date *he* knows is his birth date. It's forty-four, isn't it, Bernice?"

"Forty-four if you count the separation. Otherwise, it's forty-nine."

"So who's counting?" laughs Donald. "*Salut.*"

"*Salut.*"

Salut.

7

Bernice is in bed, sleeping late as she usually does. She is a night person, always has been. She doesn't even really get started till the sun goes down and never goes to sleep before two. Harold, on the other hand, went to bed at eleven and was up and about by six.... Differences, the things that make a difference, for better and for worse, forever.... Bernice is in that half-sleep, half-awake stage, unable to go fully back to sleep, not yet ready to get up. A surprisingly spring-like breeze wafts through her window and warms her. She reminds herself: today is the first day of spring. She breathes deeply, sighs, and begins mentally preparing her day: to have her hair done, to go to a recital at one of her former student's studio, to do the shopping for dinner, to work in the garden if there's time. She hears a noise. A tin can falling over. A yowl. A screech. Birds hawking. Stiff, she sits up slowly, stands, and walks over to the window that faces her backyard. She already knows it's Fred, her neighbor's tom, trying to catch a bird. She looks out. Sure enough, Fred is clawing his way up the oak. She looks around. On a low, thin branch sits a jay, squawking. Flying all around it is another jay, screeching, hawking, dive-bombing Fred, who doesn't seem to know whether he should go up or down the tree. "Go home, Fred! Go home!" Bernice yells. Fred scampers up the tree. Bernice puts on her bathrobe and hurries outside. When she gets there, Fred is holding the jay in his mouth, very proud. Its wings are still fluttering, feathers are flying. "Stop it, Fred!" Bernice calls as the other jay swoops down and pecks at his tail. Fred drops the jay in his mouth and swipes at the other with his paw. Bernice picks up the bird. She can feel its heart beating and the warmth of its body departing. She strokes it, soothes it, comforts it, and waits for the bird to die. Then she places it on the grass, leaving it for whatever comes next. She walks over to Fred to scold him and send him home, and sees him pawing at something on the ground. A nest. Upside down. "Go, Fred. Scat!" she sweeps with her hands, bends down, and turns it over. Inside are three dead baby jays and a live one. Gently, Bernice picks up the baby bird, holds it cupped carefully between her hands, and carries it into her house. She places it on the kitchen counter and looks at it—its clumsy feet, its tiny wings, its open mouth—and wonders what she should feed it. "What would you like to eat?" she asks as she goes to the refrigerator for some milk. The bird peeps. She takes out the milk. It peeps again. Bernice puts down the container and goes back to the counter. The bird stares at her. She stares back. Its mouth is open. It peeps. "Harold," Bernice whispers, "is that you?"

Yes.

THE SILENCE

My leg kicks and I wake with a start and lie there, still, with my eyes shut. My heart is racing and I'm covered with sweat. I reach over for Phyllis, to hold her, but she's gone. I roll back and open my eyes and lie there with my hands folded over my chest looking up at the ceiling light fixture. Then I get out of bed and get dressed and go looking for Phyllis.

I walk down the hallway carefully, quietly, looking around—as if there is something stalking me. I half expect to find Phyllis dead in the kitchen from a stroke or slumped over in the living room, bleeding. I lean around the corner and look. She's squeezed into her chair with her legs underneath her, reading, surrounded by papers and magazines and books. On the table next to her is a cantaloupe rind, two or three broken zwieback crackers, last night's empty brandy glass, and a mug full of steaming coffee. I get my cup and fill it and go sit down.

Phyllis just keeps on reading. Her eyes don't leave the page. They sweep right, left, and down, taking in whole lines at a time, half pages. She's reading faster and faster, I've noticed, and she's eating less and dieting again. Her eyes move, her fingers, her breasts and shoulders as she breathes or sighs. It amazes me how calmly she can sit there, how composed. A strand of hair slips forward, stops, comes to rest against her cheek, and she leaves it there. I get itchy just watching it. I scratch. I moan. My arm's sore.

Phyllis raises her eyes and looks at me, and I wonder: has she any idea what's happening? But I'm much too embarrassed to ask. I nod and look away. I don't want her to think I'm watching her. I don't want her to know I'm scared. I get up to refill my coffee cup. Phyllis shakes her head no without even lifting her eyes. I go into the kitchen and watch her. She used to read for an hour or so in the evening before going to sleep, then she stopped, saying she couldn't concentrate anymore, and now she's started again. Only now she reads voraciously, the way she did in college. Lately it's been D.H. Lawrence. She reads him like it's her job. I work around the house trying to keep one step ahead.

I come back with my cup full of coffee and sit down. Phyllis is still huddled in her chair. She astonishes me with her extremes. Last night in bed she was wild. Possessed. Her eyes in the moon's glow were like marbles, cat's eyes frozen in light. Her nostrils flared. Sweat ran from her forehead and down her neck. "Do it hard," she said, "as hard as you can. I want to know you've been here. I want to feel you after you've gone." I didn't know what to do. I stopped and stared at her, frightened. She dug her nails into me then and scratched and raked and gripped me with arms and legs and pushed and pulled and taunted. "Come on," she said. "Come on, *come on*! You know you want to. The way we used to when we were kids." And when I still didn't move the way she wanted, she grabbed my hair and bit my arm. I pounded her then, pounded into her, as hard as I could, crushing my bones on hers, I pounded and pounded and pounded until I couldn't breathe anymore and she screamed. Then she went to sleep, and I took one of her pills and lay there waiting for it to hit, trying hard not to think of the silence. I made a list of things to do.

I reach down and pick up the paper. Every part of me hurts. I have no idea how Phyllis can sit there, so quiet and still. She's five-foot-four and weighs 112. I'm six-foot-two and weigh 210—and I hit her with all that I had, like a tackle hitting a quarterback, smashing her,

God help me, hurting her and wanting to, and this morning I ache all over, and she's purring like a cat in the sun.

I lean back and look at my watch. "It's getting late," I say.

Phyllis says nothing.

"There's still time to go to the reservoir."

Uh-uh, she shakes her head. "You go. I want to stay here and read. I've never read any Lawrence before."

I lean forward. "It's going to rain later, you could...."

Phyllis raises her eyes and looks at me—and stares, the same way she used to look at June when June was a child and doing something she knew she shouldn't have been. I stare back, then look past her, out the window, at the oak tree we planted twenty-one years ago when we first moved into this house. Its leaves have already begun to turn, and some of them have started to fall. I get up and bring the paper back into the kitchen, I wash out my coffee cup and put it on the rack to dry. I look back in the living room at Phyllis sitting there all curled up and collected. I'm envious. If I could do it I would, but the stillness of it unnerves me.

I go out back to get the rake. Next door, Albert is doing his warm-up exercises, getting himself ready to jog. I watch him through the hedges as he does his deep knee bends and jumping jacks, as he leans against his house and stretches, then kneels, lies on his grass and sits up and down and reaches and twists and pulls an imaginary weight in the air.

I start to walk over to talk to him but stop when I hear our phone ring. I stand there and listen and wait. Ever since my mother called with the news about my father, I've come to expect the worst. There are days when Phyllis drives off to work and I think I'll never see her again. She comes to the screen door, looking agitated.

"What's wrong?" I call. I'm squeezing the rake in my hands.

"June!" she says, and my heart jumps. "She's moved the family dinner up one week."

"So what," I swallow, relieved.

"So I'm not ready. I *can't* be ready." She pulls her blouse out of her jeans and stands there pulling and tugging the tails. I don't get it. My father's half-paralyzed from a stroke, her mother's in a home, and Albert's wife Martha is dying from brain cancer—and she's upset because June is moving her wedding-dinner date up one week. "Who cares?" I say. "The sooner the better I say," and start to rake.

Phyllis puts her hands into her front pockets and balls them into fists, then pushes them down as far as they'll go. She looks like she's going to cry. I know I should go in and hug her, reassure her, tell her everything is fine and ok, that she's beautiful, lovely, sexy, and thin, but I can't. I don't have it. I'm doing all I can to keep going myself. I rake faster, digging the rake in deep, hard, yanking, piling, trying to ignore the clean fresh smell of the grass, the crackling sounds of the leaves, the odor of the earth, the dampness of it, its darkness and blankness, the way it opens when I grab it.

I look back up for Phyllis—I want to tell her everything is ok, that it will be ok, that it's all all right and there's no need to worry—but she's gone and I'm already thinking about my father and about June and how all of us, fathers and mothers and husbands and wives and daughters and sons and sisters and brothers have played in the leaves, in the grass, in the sand, in the sun, at the ocean, the bay, the park, our backyards, and I remember my dad and me making forts and how June and I made tunnels and I remember Albert and Martha having leaf fights and Phyllis and me hugging and laughing and drinking hot mulled wine in the cold night air as we stood over the crackling fire of burning leaves the very first autumn we were here. All of us so different yet the same, each of us going through everything, no one or nothing is spared. My eyes swell. It's crazy. I've thought about seeing a doctor, but what would he tell me that I don't already know: that I'm getting sentimental as I get older; that I work too much; that I need to relax and let go.

I spend the next two hours making piles of leaves, raking smaller mounds into larger mounds until I have three large mounds in the yard. I look up. The sun is still bright, but clouds are moving in and the air is beginning to chill. I shiver and button my shirt, then cover each of the mounds with plastic so they won't blow away or get wet when it rains. There was a time when I enjoyed doing this, when I thought of it as part of the seasonal change, but now it's just a chore, one more thing to finish before winter begins.

I hear the screen door open and turn around. Phyllis is standing on the top step holding a plate with a sandwich and some chips in one hand and a beer in the other. The sandwich, I know, is going to be something exotic. When Phyllis is eating, lunch is nothing but quick food, junk food, frozen food, and the commonplace–tuna, peanut butter and jelly, and bologna. When she's dieting, though, all kinds of exotic things appear. She comes down the steps and hands me the plate and together we go to the picnic table. I look at the sandwich quizzically. "Deviled crab," she says. "I made it fresh." The beer is Sam Adams, my favorite.

I offer her a bite, because crab I know is her favorite, but she covers her mouth and puffs up her cheeks and shakes her head, No. We sit there together quietly, me eating and Phyllis looking around.

"Looks good," Phyllis says after a while.

I smile. I have on my old, torn Pendleton, my hair is a mess, there's mud on my pants, dirt on my face, and I'm sticky and smelly from sweat. "Me?" I say, "or the yard?"

"The yard," she laughs, reaching out and straightening my hair. I take her hand and hold it. I know why she touched my hair–and why now she's looking at my mouth. I see the same things too–in her eyes, her hands, her legs, her shoulders. "Done?" she asks, and I nod. She picks up the plate and walks back to the house. I keep my eyes on her shoulders, then her legs, until she opens the screen door and vanishes. It's only about ninety feet and it takes less than fifteen seconds, but it feels like twenty centuries. Who determines what gets passed on, I wonder? Which of me will return as it is and which will be newly mixed in June's children and her children's children and so on? What secret parts will be rediscovered—and what happens to those that are lost?

It's after two, but I'm not ready to return to the house. I put the rake back in the toolshed and go to the garage to work on the storms. They're exactly where I left them six months ago—neatly stacked and in order against the far wall. I go over and look at them: Tthe windows are spider-webby and pitted with mildew; some of the frames are beginning to rot. I take the living-room windows from the first stack and start working on them. I work until the phone rings, then I stop and wait, and when Phyllis doesn't call me I go back to working again. I work until it's almost dark, then put everything back the way it was and go inside.

Something delicious is cooking, I smell it as soon as I open the door. I go to the bathroom to shower and clean up, then wrap a towel around me and go looking for Phyllis. She's back in her chair, coiled up, still reading. I'm about to ask her what smells so good, but she doesn't look up so I go back to the bedroom to dress. Phyllis follows a few minutes later and nestles in behind me while I button my shirt. She pulls it out as I tuck it in.

"Velma Washington's at Billie's tonight," she says. "Let's go."

"Billie's?" I repeat

"Uh-huh."

"You want to go to Billie's?" I tuck in my shirt.

She nods.

"And hear Velma Washington?"

"Sure."

"*You* want to hear the blues?"

Phyllis laughs and pulls out my shirt. Everything about her lately surprises me.

I'm waiting in the foyer for Phyllis. She's still in the bedroom dressing. It's another of our differences that's growing. I'm getting ready earlier and earlier and Phyllis is taking her time. I hear the bedroom door close, the sound of her shoes in the hallway. I look up. She's wearing a new buckskin jacket and jeans, black high heels, a black and red scarf, black blouse, and the diamond teardrop earrings I gave her for our last anniversary. "Looking good," I say, "looking good." I'm wearing my old standbys: plaid flannel shirt, jeans, jean jacket, and cowboy boots.

"I'll drive," she says before we even get out the door. I look at her and frown. I don't like her car, and I don't like to be driven, and she knows it. She walks past me, gets into her car and starts the engine. I lock the house and go to her car and look through the passenger window. My side is covered with moldy styrofoam coffee cups, faded newspapers, encrusted candy wrappers, and a half-eaten rotting peach. Phyllis reaches over and opens the door. "Just toss it in back," she says. I look at her in disbelief, then toss it all and sit down. The car reeks. It smells putrid. I lower the window and stick my head out, then I lock the door and buckle up. I want to get there as fast as I can.

Phyllis pulls out of the driveway and pushes a tape into her tape deck and I listen, surprised, as Bessie Smith begins to sing. I look at Phyllis, who looks back at me and smiles. Then I look in her tape box and see that all of the tapes are mine: country, blues, gospel—

music I could never get her to listen to. We drive all the way to Billie's listening to Bessie sing and get there in time to get a table.

I order Wild Turkey for myself and a vodka collins for Phyllis. She looks at me as if I'm being presumptuous, then shrugs. We settle in and listen to the house band and wait for Velma. The band isn't bad, and I feel wonderful sitting there with the good music, good whiskey, and my wife. I take Phyllis's hand and hold it, and she taps her foot on the floor. I look around for our waitress, to order another round before it gets really busy, and see Albert and Martha sitting at a table with two couples on the other side of the room. Phyllis also sees them and waves. "Albert called," she says. "He said they'd be here if Martha was feeling ok."

Feeling ok! She looks incredible—tanned, healthy, trim, full of life. She's laughing and giggling hysterically, holding her belly with one hand and pulling on Albert's arm with the other to get him to stand up and dance. I'm amazed. Ever since she was diagnosed, I've been watching her, to see what she sees, what she knows, what secrets have been revealed to her. I don't understand how she can go on day after day, doing what she's always done, knowing she's about to die. I watch her and she's the same Martha—same huge wild laugh and silly puns. She still works in her garden, reads, exercises, and comes to places like Billie's. If it was me, I'd quit my job and travel, search the world for cures. I keep looking over at them and at Phyllis, who's ordered her third drink now and become quieter as the audience gets noisier waiting for Velma.

She finally appears and I can't believe it. She must weigh two hundred pounds and be over seventy years old, and she's squeezed into an amazingly tight red and silver sequined dress—but there's no doubt about it, the lady can still sing. She opens with "Sweet Georgia Brown" and takes me back to when I was a boy.

Halfway through the first set, a young woman—a girl really, about the same age as June—gets up and starts to dance by herself. It's the most sensual thing I've witnessed. She moves like a snake, from the inside out, as if something way down deep inside of her just started undulating and rippling its way through her skin. Everyone sits riveted, the women as well as the men, and it reminds me of June and how she dances, and of Phyllis and how she did too, and I wonder if strange men look at my daughter and think what I'm thinking as I look at this girl? Phyllis touches me–my mouth, my ear, runs her fingers through my hair. I close my eyes, it feels so good. Then I open them when Velma sings, "Willow Weep for Me," and I see that Phyllis is crying. "Why the tears?" I ask. She doesn't answer. "Phyllis, why are you crying?"

"For me," she says. "I'm crying for me."

I take her hand and pull her from her chair and hold her. I wrap my arms around her and hold her tight, squeezing her to me and kissing her hair, her head, her neck, her shoulders. To everyone around us we're dancing–but I know and Phyllis knows we're holding on for dear life.